George Hughes Hepworth

Starboard and Port

George Hughes Hepworth

Starboard and Port

ISBN/EAN: 9783337042097

Printed in Europe, USA, Canada, Australia, Japan

Cover: Foto ©Andreas Hilbeck / pixelio.de

More available books at **www.hansebooks.com**

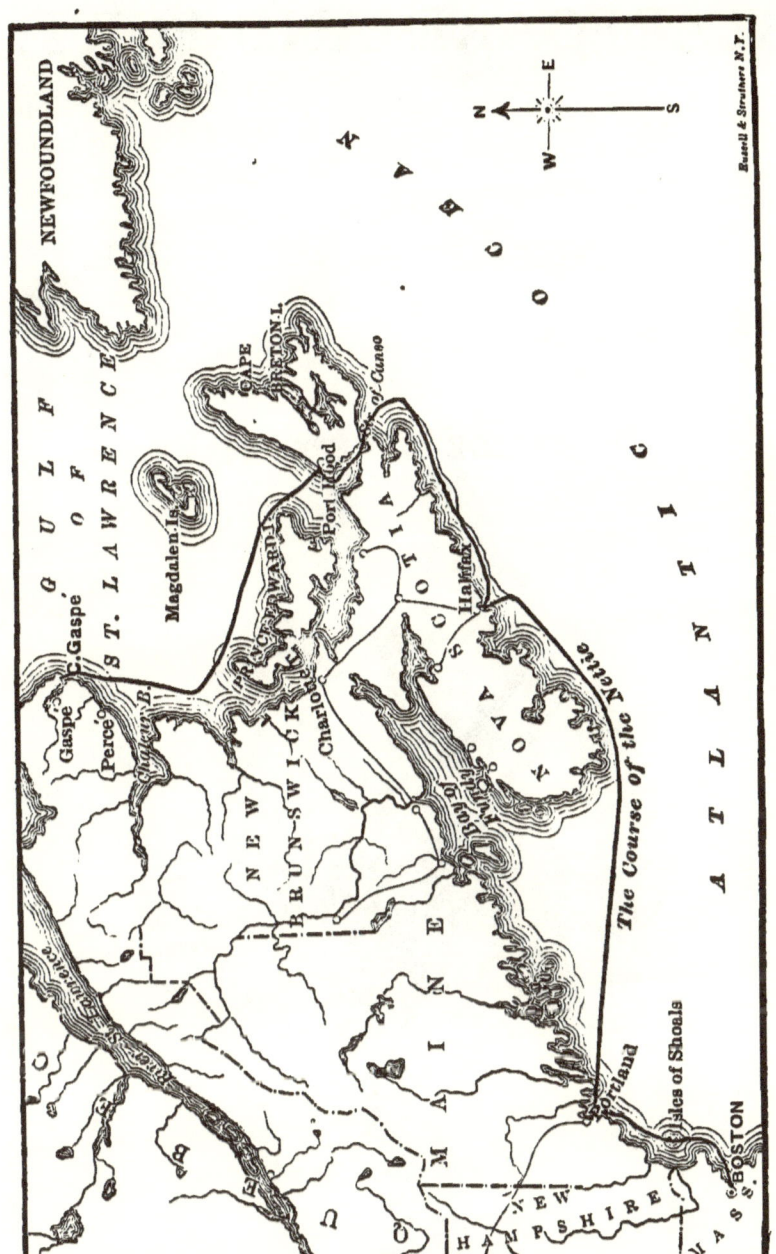

The Nettie's Course.

STARBOARD AND PORT:

THE "NETTIE" ALONG SHORE.

By GEORGE H. HEPWORTH.

NEW YORK:

HARPER & BROTHERS, PUBLISHERS,

FRANKLIN SQUARE.

1876.

TO

AMBROSE A. RANNEY, Esq.,

(RULOFF)

WHO HAS BEEN TO ME FOR NEARLY TWENTY YEARS WHAT MAN

RARELY FINDS, AND WHAT HE PRIZES WHEN HE FINDS,

A TRUE FRIEND;

AND HIS BROTHER, J. W. RANNEY, M.D.,

EQUALLY MY FRIEND,

I Dedicate this Book.

G. H. H.

PREFACE.

In a work so unpretending as this a Preface is hardly needed. My book would never have seen the light but for the kindness of friends. They listened so patiently to my repeated recitals of adventure that I was tempted to seek a larger audience. I have had three objects in view in elaborating my log: First, the happiness it always gives me to talk about the ocean; second, the hope of giving pleasure to others; and, third, my desire to induce yachtsmen to venture into blue water. If I fail in the last, I shall fall back cheerfully to the other two; and if the second be unattainable, then the pleasure I have had in writing the book remains, and I am quite content.

I desire to give public expression of my gratitude to the Rev. M. Harvey, of St. John's, Newfoundland, who sent me maps and public documents concerning an island which offers special inducements to the angler, the hunter, and the explorer—which island I hope to visit some day, when I shall be under still greater obligations for his kindness; also to the Massachusetts Arms Manufacturing Company of Chicopee, Mass., which very generously presented me with a couple of the justly celebrated Maynard rifles for my expedition. I had the pleasure of using them on some small game, and am perfectly willing to trust them against larger game when the opportunity shall present itself.

And so I launch my little craft into what I hope will prove to be the sea of a kind and friendly criticism.

G. H. H.

TABLE OF CONTENTS.

"Thalatta! Thalatta!
I greet thee, thou Ocean Eternal!
I give thee ten thousand times greeting,
   With heart all exulting,
   As, ages since, hailed thee
   Those ten thousand Greek hearts—
Fate-conquering, home-yearning,
World-renowned Greek hearts.

"The billows were rolling,
   Were rolling and roaring,
The sun poured downward incessant,
The flickering rose-lights;
Affrighted, the flocks of the sea-mews
Fluttered away, loud-screaming;
The steeds were stamping, the shields were clanging,
And far, like a shout of victory, echoed
   Thalatta! Thalatta!"
                              HEINE.

"Thou Ocean Eternal, I greet thee!
Like the tongue of my home is the dash of thy waters!
Like dreams of my childhood now sparkle before me
All the wide-curving waves of thy rolling dominions."
                              HEINE.

"Good-bye to Pain and Care! I take
   Mine ease to-day;
Here where these sunny waters break,
And ripples this keen breeze, I shake
All burdens from my heart, all weary thoughts away."
                              WHITTIER.

CHAPTER I.

GETTING READY.

HERE is no love so absorbing as a love of the ocean, and there are few pleasures in life half so sweet as drifting on the current or facing the gale in a trim, well-built, and weatherly yacht. The land has its charms indeed, but blue water is a constant and soul-satisfying fascination. In the landscape you have always the same outlines, however various may be the light and shadow, the gloom and sunshine which fill up the picture ; but on the ocean the scene is changed not only with every change of wind, but with the ever-varying force of the wind. In the morning you have the gentle zephyr, just filling your sails and curling the water into little fantastic ripples which rise and fall on the regular swell with the perfect rhythm of poetry, and in the afternoon a heavy blow from the east, coming like a giant with his whip and driving the frightened waves before him until they rise from the surface in snow-capped ridges, all the while muttering their deep - voiced mournful music, which just colors your consciousness of the grandeur of the picture with a pale shade of fear. At one time the clouds seem to be looking at themselves as though the sea were a mirror, and you watch the shadows as they play at hide-and-seek with something of the interest with which you watch the moods of a child's face; then from horizon to horizon, unbroken by intruding island or rock, stretches the sombre gray which makes you feel that Nature herself is sad. At another time the sky, absolutely cloudless, shines like burnished silver, into which has been thrown the faintest possible reflection of blue, while the heat pours down with torrid power; then you rise and fall on the watery undulations, and your reefing-points rap the sails with a conscious impatience. You are reminded of the Ancient Mariner, and imagine yourself in a painted ship on a painted ocean. Ah! there is nothing half so sweet in life as a full, deep, and open-souled communion with the sea.

It seems to me, however, that yachting in America has hardly reached the dignity it possesses in England. We Americans play on the water, while the English live on it. It is with us the sport of an afternoon, and consists, in its most extended expression, of a trip along the shore of Long Island. Our craft seldom venture on long voyages, and would do themselves little credit in a northeast gale. They have generally very graceful lines, great breadth of beam, which makes them roomy and comfortable under deck, but are often so overloaded with spars and canvas that they are unfit for rough outside work. In our whole fleet there are hardly half a dozen boats which an old sailor would pronounce snugly trimmed. The main-boom runs outboard as though the mast had fallen over the stern, and when the yacht is flying before a ten-knot breeze the foot of the mainsail slaps the water, and makes such a swash that all the comfort of sailing is changed into anxiety for the rigging. Our topmasts, too, run up to such an incredible height that when the boat begins to roll in a sea-way it seems as though she would never stop until she had jerked out her spars.

I am ready to admit that our American yachts are the most graceful pieces of marine architecture in existence. Nothing can exceed the beauty of a regatta off Sandy Hook in a six or eight knot breeze. The white-winged craft skim over the water like the flight of gulls, while the hulls lose themselves in clouds of spotless canvas. It is an infinite pity, however, that their mission ends when the wind increases, and that before the stiff breeze which the fisherman or the pilot-boat only laughs at, they creep under a lee for safety. The truth is, they are built to look at, but not to last. That part of the hull which is seen is carefully looked after, but that part which is under the water-line is left to neglect. The average yacht is hermetically sealed by the builder, and ventilation regarded as entirely unnecessary. The Gloucester fisherman pickles his vessel, and leaves air-holes in every possible corner. He fills the space between the plank and the ceiling with salt clear up to the deck, and as a consequence his craft when fifteen or twenty years old is as solid as when she came off the stocks. Our yachtsmen forget that a boat is like the human lungs—it must have air, or it will surely rot. A well-known ship-builder told me the other day that most of our yachts which are more than five years old have passed their usefulness. They are likely to be pricked both at the stern and in the run, the two places in a boat which it is most difficult to ventilate. I have known a single race to so strain a yacht that it became necessary to haul her up on the ways and put the caulkers on her bottom. The truth is, we are consumed by a madness for speed, and every thing is sacrificed to that one quality. To make the best time is all we care for. We can run all round an English yacht in fair weather and smooth water, but when we are caught in a gale, and have to lie-to for a couple of days, the Englishman eats his meals in serenity, assured that his boat will ride it out, while we chew the cud of discontent and look wistfully toward home. It has made me groan sometimes to see a fleet outside of the Hook taking in its kites or luffing up to reef in nothing more than an honest wholesale breeze, while an outward-bound pilot-boat, carrying all its canvas, bowled along as though it were only playing with the wind.

The crowning defect, and one which we are beginning to acknowledge, is the shape of the bows. They are so sharp that they not only cut through the water when it is smooth, but they also cut into it and under it when there is any sea-way on. The only thing that holds the head of a yacht up in rough weather is its preposterous bowsprit and jib-boom. The fisherman is so fashioned above the water-line forward that when she dives into a sea she has wood enough to keep her on top of the water. There is so much wood and so much breadth by the cat-heads that when she plunges, she instantly rises, while the yacht, which has no wood forward, and is as sharp as a knife, plunges and stays there until her deck as far aft as the fore-rigging is all under water. As an inevitable consequence, the whole head-gear is endangered at a time when the pilot-boat goes laughingly by with dry decks.

A few of our larger craft are notable exceptions to this rule. The *Sappho*, the *Dauntless*, the *Enchantress*, the *Dreadnought*, and some others, are perhaps not open to the criticisms I have made. And yet even these yachts are built so sharp that in an ordinary chop sea outside they run their noses under water in a very disagreeable way, imperiling their whole head-gear. They are all something over two hundred tons' burden, cost almost fabulous sums, and ought to be able to round the Horn as comfortably and safely as a full-rigged ship; and yet they are not the vessels in which an old salt would feel secure. It is not the mahogany, rosewood, plate-glass, and general extravagance of outfit which frightens him, but the low bow and rail, the wedge-like prow which lets the water come aboard instead of dashing it aside, and which is so thin and sharp that there is scarcely any lifting quality in the boat except when the jib-boom and bowsprit strike the wave and buoy her up. Any yacht that measures a hundred tons, that has seventy-five feet of deck-room, ought to be able to go the wide world over, and to take whatever might come. With lower masts and shorter spars the sails could be snugly trimmed close to the deck; and though something might be lost in speed, an enormous gain of safety would give an enviable and manly dignity to American yachting. Besides — and this is a consideration not to be despised—we should

become a hardier and more venturesome race of boat-
men, and spend our summers in distant waters, and in
the acquisition of marine prowess—a quality of character in which we are sadly deficient. Long Island
Sound is the disease of which we are dying. To that are
we indebted for that evil invention, the centre-board.
It has taught us to dread Cape Cod; and with its
smoother water has taken the life out of our love for
the ocean, and substituted the fascinations of a mill-
pond. We crawl along inshore, and run for a harbor
when the wind blows a reefing breeze. The play
of a coaster or lumberman is the agony of a yacht.
We are oppressed with the consciousness that our boats
are not weatherly; that we have paid too much for
brass and mahogany, and too little for good solid oak;
that we have sacrificed every thing to a knife-like bow
and fifteen knots an hour; and so we shake the rope's
end in the face of a Banker when we pass him this
side of Newport, but dare not for our lives follow him
to the big waves of the fishing-ground.

Now, if the only object of yachting is a few hours'
pleasure, that end is fully met by the present condition of affairs. It is certainly delightful, when one
is sitting on the piazza of his sea-side home, to gaze at
the graceful boat riding safely at anchor a hundred
yards from shore. It tingles one's nervous system to
look at the trig uniforms of the sailors, and hear the
mellow tones of the bell when it strikes the hour.
Besides, there is a certain glamour about owning a yacht
—every body regards it as a bit of fairy-land, and looks
with inexpressible envy on the Yacht Club buttons and
the gay colors of the signal code, and the wreathing

smoke as the miniature gun announces that the great sun has set for the day, but proposes to rise and smile on the well-painted craft on the morrow. I am willing to confess that all this is exceedingly pleasant, but after all it is only a sort of fresh-water experience, and after a while one tires of it. It does very well for the first year, but after that the appetite is cloyed, and we need something more stimulating.

I have a strong conviction that yachting may be made, and will yet become, a very much more important matter than it is at present. It is only a pastime just now, but years hence it will become an element of national strength. What West Point is for the land, yachting ought to be for the water—an education that may some time stand the country in good stead. Just now our yacht-owners leave their business at three o'clock in the afternoon, take a turn round Southwest Spit, or possibly run out to the Lightship, and that is all. Their yachts, like their carriages, are governed by a hired man. Now I do not intend to discourage the pursuit of pleasure, or to find unnecessary fault. I am simply trying to look at matters squarely, and to tell the plain truth. I will not go so far as some writers, and say that no man has a right to ride unless he can drive his own horses, and none a right to sail unless, at least in an emergency, he can command his own craft; but I have a very earnest feeling that we are playing at yachting, and reaching after no special good. If we can get nothing more out of our boats than an occasional sail among the drift-wood of the harbor, then we will be content with that; but if we can be roused to something better and more worthy of our national prestige, then welcome the voice that scolds for our good.

I think I see what this pleasure may become in the future, and am somewhat impatient perhaps for the consummation. Our yacht models have in times past had a great influence on the merchant marine. They have put to the blush those old square-headed vessels which used literally to fight their way across the ocean, and one by one they have disappeared from our waters. Now we have ships more comely in shape, more fleet of foot, and equally useful for purposes of trade. But of late years yachts have become toys, and lost their prestige as teachers. They have very little, if any thing, to do with progress in marine architecture, and are looked upon as simply an extravagance in cost, shape, and canvas.

I am looking forward hopefully to the time when our fleet will not anchor at Newport. The Sound is the primary school, while Cape Cod is the high school of American yachtsmen. We have solved the problem of speed, and can shoot over smooth water like a ricochetting bullet. With centre-board up when running before the wind, we can beat the world. The next question to be settled, and the far more important one, is the question of weatherly qualities. If we should dare to run our fleet into the teeth of a downright northeaster, we might rattle every thing to pieces, but we should return wiser for the experience, and, I doubt not, resolved on a radical change. There is so much that is admirable in this national determination to do the best thing that can be done, that I feel very sure the whole character of yachting is to suffer a change of base in the next ten years. We shall yet have the best sea-boats as well as the fastest craft of which any people can boast, and we shall yet be as proud of the way in which our vessels will fight a gale as we are now of the swiftness with which they glide over smooth water.

The ideal model is in the future. The English yacht is altogether too clumsy, and the American altogether too tender. The Englishman is narrow and deep; the American wide and flat. It is not impossible to combine the best qualities of these two styles, and then we shall leave the Sound and take to deep water.

I sent the *Nettie*, late in June, to New London, to have her masts cut down and her main-boom shortened. The sticks were preposterously long, and made her roll badly in a heavy swell, while the main-boom ran outboard so far that, when the wind was on the quarter and she was running free, the end of it dipped as she swayed, and threatened to carry away the masthead. She was in good trim for racing in smooth water, and had many a time shown her wake to her rivals, so it went hard with me to alter her proportions; but I thought of the Nova Scotia coast, and the "harricanes" which seem to have their own way with our stanch fishing-smacks even, and concluded to sacrifice something to comfort and safety. She would have to meet whatever might come, and would need to be strong in every timber and line. She was carefully examined in the hull, all her running rigging was overhauled, and every thing done to fit her for the hard work which lay before us.

We went on board in Boston harbor July 6th. The

yacht looked ready for any thing, and seemed to have
a half consciousness that she was on the edge of a new
experience, and that great things were expected.   It is
no small task to prepare for a voyage.   Our steward
was busy getting the saloon and state-rooms in readiness, and it devolved upon me to buy the provisions.
Never having had to look after a large family, I made
a great many blunders.   I sent Algar in one direction
to search for water and ice; Bertric in another direction, to purchase flour and potatoes; Stigand in still
another, to buy meat for the hands and steaks for the
cabin; and reserved to myself the duty of gathering
together the odds and ends which go so far to make up
the comfort of a cruise.   My little army defiled from
the wharf, and soon each individual needle was finding
a different way through the human haystack.   In the
course of a couple of hours spent in a weary search
after mustard and gherkins and fancy crackers, I found
my slow and hot way along the lower part of the city,
my arms piled full of small bundles, which seemed to
have no coherency whatever; for first one parcel would
drop, involving the necessity of laying down nearly all
the rest in order to pick that one up, and then another
parcel, which did not appear to enjoy its proximity to
its neighbor, started off from the top of the pile, as a
small avalanche from a mountain-top, and slid down to
the sidewalk, bringing up with such a force that the
paper burst, and half the contents were spilled.   The
small boy behind me, who was carrying his bundles
very comfortably in a basket, seemed to enjoy the experience more than I did.   If it had been cool, I could
have kept my temper; but with the mercury among

the nineties, it was more than human patience could bear; so, objurgating that steward in a mild set of epithets which were more indicative of sorrow than of anger, I sat down on the doorstep of a warehouse, with the impression that all inanimate things are totally depraved. Just then a troop of hangers-on, looking out for a petty job, discovered my predicament. They rushed at me, vociferously demanding the privilege of carrying my bundles for me. A half-dozen of them grabbed a parcel each, and in single file, a stately and august procession, they marched down to the boat,

while I loitered behind, a victim of untoward circumstances. After the bundles had been delivered to the
sailors, mostly in a state of dilapidation, each bundle
having done its best to leak itself away, my convoys
gathered in a semicircle about me, and asked remuner-
ation for their valuable services. I gave them a quarter apiece, and found that the articles aggregated a
very handsome sum, of which the cartage was the principal item.

Bertric had arrived in a very moist condition, but
with his freight in good order, since, with characteristic
caution, he had hired an express wagon. We waited
impatiently for thirty minutes the arrival of the other
two members of the company, when I indiscreetly suggested the propriety of entering upon a tour of discovery. It seemed a very simple thing to do, and also an
act of friendship toward our comrades, who might be
lost amid the tangled streets of the city. So I started
in the direction which Algar ought to have taken, while
Bertric went in search of Stigand. We afterward
learned from the sailors that Algar and Stigand arrived
a few minutes after our departure, and immediately set
out in search of us. An hour and a half was thus
spent in a very successful game of hide-and-seek, which
would have been tolerable if our object had been to
escape one another, but which was entirely unsatisfac-
tory since our object was to find one another.

Let me, however, draw the curtain of forgetfulness
over that season of bitter wandering, and come to the
pleasant fact that at three o'clock, after the wind, which
had been favorable all the morning, had died out altogether, and the tide had begun to flow, we met with a

fond embrace, our list of provisions was complete, and our tempers in the sulkiest possible mood.

We were rowed out to the yacht, which lay a couple of chains off, passed the stores to the steward, and unanimously expressed the opinion that the whole experience, though somewhat novel, was not on the whole of the most agreeable kind. The boats were swung to the davits, the anchor was hove short, the sail - stops were unbound, the halyards were manned, and the white canvas swayed up to the merry song of the sailors. We were ready at last.

Just then a light air filled the sails, the anchor was hove chock a-block, the order was given to up with the jib, and the *Nettie*, hesitating a moment, as though to say good-bye to friendly waters, shot away from her moorings, and we were off.

Boston has certainly a picturesque harbor. The city, as seen from a distance, is very attractive; and the islands, which serve as so many breakwaters, each one forming a lee, help to make a very impressive picture. We glided by Fort Independence, and the never-to-be-finished fort on Governor's Island, by Long Island, with the Inner Light on its eastern front, by Nix Mate, and so out by way of Broad Sound. We were then fairly at sea, of which fact we were reminded by the gentle undulation which was the remnant of the last heavy blow.

There was hardly any breeze, and our progress was consequently slow. We made only about four knots, but the night was superb. The great army of stars came out, crowding and hustling one another as though they had human passions, and were all bent on an eager mission. The lights along the coast slowly

faded into the dim distance : first Nahant, then Bever-
ly, then Lynn, then Gloucester, after which we made
for the double lights of Cape Ann. Once by those,
we could lay our course for Star Island Light, with the
lights off Portsmouth on the far larboard. It seemed
impossible to sleep, so we sat up on deck, admiring the
scene, each in his own way.

The heavens seem very friendly to one on the water,
and the sailor never tires of watching the stars. The
man at the wheel generally picks out a prominent one
to steer by, only casting an occasional glance at the
compass to assure himself that the two guides cor-
respond. It is not very easy for thoughtful men to
have a rattling time at night on board a vessel. They
may scintillate occasionally, throwing off a spark of
wit, but the integral influence of the ocean is subduing.
It leads to reverie and introspection. Ruloff spent the
evening forward among the sailors, listening to the experiences which they delight to narrate, and almost always in a quiet and impressive sort of way. The rest
of us were seated in the cockpit, talking with the man
at the wheel, and making plans for the future.

Our view of the comet was something wonderful.
There was a thin haze for a few degrees above the
horizon, but for a couple of hours the mysterious messenger held his equal way through the clear ether, and
showed his magnificent proportions to great advantage. A nodule of fire served as a kind of figure-head,
from which swept that amazing trail of light at which
a wondering world was looking. While I sat absorbed
and silent, Ah Boo, our Mongolian, to whose keeping
we had intrusted the important duty of overseeing the

culinary department, emerged from his laboratory to get a breath of air. He stared about the sky until he came to the comet, and then his surprise and wonder reached their climax. The erratic messenger was evidently a novelty to his untutored mind, and he broke forth in an apostrophe, which may have been very eloquent in Chinese, but which was sufficiently unintelligible as English.

"Come, come!" he said, as he took me by the sleeve and hurried me across the deck to the fore-rigging, "Mr. Hepper, see! star all in a smoke of fire! What the matter? you know?"

I assured the simple fellow that I really did not know the exact condition of affairs up there; when, seeing that I was undisturbed, he concluded that there was no occasion for immediate alarm, and quietly emptied his bucket, which he had been most pertinaciously and unconsciously holding, and, with more subdued eloquence in an unknown tongue, re-entered the abyss of the cook-room, and was lost to view.

That same evening I saw a more brilliant meteor than it had ever been my lot to behold. I suppose phenomena of equal brilliancy are often visible in other quarters of the globe, but this one was so startlingly bright that I was amazed and delighted. It was just above the starboard bow. I was looking up in meditative mood, when I saw what I took to be the fiery ball of a rocket. It was a node of white light, following just about the parabola which a rocket would naturally take. After it had traversed what seemed to be two or three degrees, it suddenly burst, and went out in darkness, leaving behind small pear-shaped brilliants, which remained for several seconds, and then disappeared.

And so the silent, still night wore on. At about one in the morning we passed the Cape Ann lights, giving them a good berth, out of respect to a ledge which lies off E.S.E. from Thatcher's Island a couple of miles, and then laid our course a little to the westward of Star Island, when, overcome with sleep, we all went to bed.

The *Nettie* is a very roomy boat, and though there were six of us in the cabin, we were all comfortably bestowed. Ruloff took the starboard state-room, filling it with guns and fishing-rods; I had the port state-room, with wash-room attached; while Algar,

Stigand, Bertric, and Fletch occupied spacious berths in the main saloon.

In the morning when we awoke we were riding at anchor among familiar and friendly craft, in front of the Appledore House, at the Isles of Shoals.

CHAPTER II.

A SPLENDID RUN.

"I never think without a thrill
Of wild and pure delight
Of all the leagues of blue, blue sea,
Which I have sailed o'er merrily
In day, or dead of night."—FABER.

HE Isles of Shoals consist of a group of bare rocks, which evidently rebelled against the geological tyranny of the past, and succeeded in just getting their heads above water. They are very unique in appearance, having been doomed, apparently in punishment for their disobedience in not staying below, to have few of the peculiar features of ordinary *terra firma*. They are no more nor less than a reef which has pushed its way up above the surface, and which pays for its rashness by being compelled to suffer the same jagged and angular and irregular appearance which its less successful neighbors in the depths possess. There is but one tree on the group, and that shoots up through the piazza of the Appledore Hotel, as though the islands were, after a sort, unfriendly to it.

Compelled to postpone our start on account of the fog, we resigned ourselves with good grace to the pleasures of this novel spot for twenty-four hours. I was myself quite at home there, for I had spent many a week in roving about on Star, Smutty Nose, Londoners, and Duck, and in a thousand and one excursions after all sorts of fish. Of course I hastened at once to pay my regards to Mrs. Thaxter, who holds a kind of court in her cottage during the summer season, and whose name has become a household word with those who love the songs of the sea. In her poems there is the peculiar and refreshing fragrance and exhilaration of salt air. She is exceedingly accessible, and has a genial welcome for all the crowd of great and little who pay their tribute of respect to her genius.

In the afternoon we all went over to Duck, about a mile from Appledore, a spot that is redolent of the memory of shipwrecks and ghouls, and all kinds of uncanny adventures. We took our lines with us, and caught sea-perch until we were tired of hauling them in, and then loaded our guns for medrakes. They are a very cunning bird, and can be shot, in this place at least, only by stratagem. When we landed, the picket-guard of these beauties, whose wings we were in search of, gave the alarm, and soon the whole army, scattered in graceful groups over the island, took flight, and flew in circles above us, screaming out their defiance. Higher and higher they soared, until they seemed but specks of white above our heads. We sat down on the rocks to wait for their descent, and our patience was soon rewarded by seeing first one and then another lower his flight, as though prompted by a dangerous curiosity to see who we were.

When they were within a reasonable shooting distance I let off a barrel, with the expectation of doing execution at the next shot. At the explosion the birds were apparently convinced either that we had no more powder or that we were bad marksmen, and that they were consequently safe, so they fluttered at short range all around us. That is the time to do your work. Three discharges, and three birds fell. The whole flock then gathered to see what was the matter, and a couple more discharges gave us all the birds we wanted. We despoiled them of their wings, and after a pleasant row heard the welcome call to supper on the part of our Mongolian.

On Saturday morning we let off our guns as a good-bye to the islanders, who were not yet up, and started for Boone Island, expecting to lay our course from that point to Seal Island, on the S.W. end of Nova Scotia. We had about four hundred miles before us, with all the delightful uncertainties of a long trip at sea. The wind, which is always persistently wrong, favored us as we sailed away from the Shoals, and then left us when we were off Boone. All that day there was a dead calm. We tried to break the monotony of ennui by fishing, but only dogfish rewarded our toil. We brought out the checker-board, and challenged each other; we listened to sailors' yarns, and told yarns ourselves; but, somehow, that regular and awful swell which came from the eastward unfitted us for long enjoyment of any thing, and produced a certain restlessness which is a symptom of inward distress. Boone Island seemed to be a magnet, and we a toy vessel with which it was playing. At ten in the morning it stood to the eastward; at twelve it stood to the southeast; at three in the afternoon it stood to the south; at five it stood to the southwest; and at sundown it stood almost directly west. We had spent the whole day in sailing, or rather in drifting around it, and were never so thankful as when darkness shut down and covered up the tower. But even then the light shone across the waters at us with an unnatural brilliancy, to remind us that it still held us in place.

> "And evening's breath, wandering here and there
> Over the quivering surface of the stream,
> Wakes not one ripple from its summer dream."
>
> SHELLEY.

There is nothing quite so demoralizing as a dead calm. A blow is exhilarating, exciting, and calls up the nervous energy of a man; but a calm cuts deep into his nature, and lets out every thing in his soul that is sour. We were not exactly seasick, but we were miserable. When Ah Boo, who was as chipper as ever, called us to dinner, we answered the summons in a sluggish sort of way, as though it were a matter of indifference to us whether we ever ate again or not. We went into the saloon, however, and most positively asserted to each other our entire freedom from any disagreeable symptoms whatever. We did our utmost to be cheerful, but there was very evidently a serious cast to all our thoughts. When the soup was spilled in some one's lap as the *Nettie* rolled, no one laughed; and if you had looked into our eyes at that moment you would have discovered a certain vacancy, as though the interior man were busy looking after his own welfare, and had no interest in external things. Indeed, an Atlantic swell, when there is no breeze to steady the vessel, is entirely *sui generis,* and must be experienced to be understood. No description can do it justice. It rolls the boat in the direction of the starboard, reserving a faint lurch toward the larboard; then, reversing the motion, it rolls the boat toward the larboard quarter, giving it at the same time a lurch toward the starboard; and at last, as though in a quandary, or suffering from indecision, it makes a

tangled snarl of every conceivable kind of motion, the general and total effect of which on the nervous system, and especially on the digestive apparatus, is far, I may say, very far from agreeable.

When in their normal condition, men on board ship are gregarious. They make friends quickly, and, getting together in select groups, chat the hours away as easily as a rivulet ripples over the stones ; but when the condition of affairs is such as I have described, they avoid each other with a mutual persistency that is very suggestive. A man who feels every time the vessel sinks under his feet as though a sudden vacuum had been produced in the region of the stomach, and who puts his hands on that part of his anatomy with an instinctive dread lest it may have been displaced, is generally in such a reflective mood that he does not take readily

to the cheering words of those who have been hardened
to that experience, but with a forced and somewhat
sickly smile expresses a wish to be undisturbed while
he follows out a train of abstruse thought.

Well, at last the day wore out, and the time arrived
to make up the slate for the night, and to set the watch.
I always work when on board the yacht, taking my turn
at the fore and my trick at the wheel, and the an-
nouncement of this purpose decided the others to do
the same. It fell to Bertric and myself to watch on
deck from twelve to six, and so I lay down at nine for
a nap. When I was called, I heard the rain pattering
on the deck, while the same old rat-tat-too of the reefing-points showed that the calm had not ended. I
walked the deck for a couple of hours, covered all up in
water-proof, when I heard a noise forward which attracted my attention. At that time the *Nettie* was
rolling in the most reckless way possible. The main-
boom had a strong guy on it, but in spite of all it slat-
ted until it seemed as though it would tear the very
masts out of her. If there had been a breath of wind
only, our sails aloft would have steadied her, but a
feather dropped from the hand would have fallen at
your feet, so still it was.

Going forward, I noticed that Bertric was leaning
over the starboard rail, apparently contemplating the
water. He was so thoroughly absorbed that when I
spoke he failed to answer. I spoke again, and still no
answer. Then I turned away, knowing that one fellow-
being at least was in misery—a misery too deep for
ordinary utterance. A while after I saw him sitting
disconsolate on the bow, and said,

"My dear fellow, how do you like yachting?"

"Like it?" he replied; "I hardly think I should venture to use that word. However, I am a wiser and sadder man just now than ever before. My first impressions of this thing are somewhat modified, and I think I should give rather a different definition to the word than that I have been accustomed to."

"Ah! well, how would you define it under the light of your present experiences?"

"I should say of yachting," he answered, in tones slow and measured, and not altogether cheerful, "that it consists in getting up at twelve, and keeping watch until six, in a dead calm, with a heavy groundswell, and a fearfully unhappy revolution going on inside, to which death seems like the sleep of a child."

He then relapsed into his introspective mood once more, and I left him to his meditations.

Thinking to cheer him up, it came into my heart to give him a serenade. So holding on to the shrouds to keep myself steady, I began, in a voice vigorous, if not musical, that song which is a precious piece of deception to landsmen:

> "A life on the ocean wave,
> A home on the *rolling* deep."

Bertric caught the tones of my voice, when I first opened this sort of vocal cannonade, and when I sang the fifth word of the second line—I think I must have dwelt on it for a couple of beats longer than the time usually allotted to it—I heard coming through the darkness a sort of sigh, which deepened into a moan, evidently a feeble response from the fore-chains. When I had finished, I was surprised to see Bertric with a great effort, and with a face too awry for happiness, standing on his feet as though he intended to return my favor. Pretty soon I heard in feeble tones, which sounded more like a hollow and mocking echo than any thing else, these words:

> "A life on the ocean wave,
> [Pause, as though undecided to continue.]
> The—man—that writ it was green;
> He never had been to sea,
> And never a gale had seen."
> [Suppressed "Oh, goodness!"]

After which, in a voice too pathetic for description, came these lines:

> "He never had seen a poor fellow
> Growing thinner every day; [Pause.]
> A-sittin' down by the forrard chock,
> And throwin' himself away." ["Oh! oh! oh!"]

I saw that the case was a hopeless one, that my friend was in a frame of mind to which solitude was the only balm, and so walked aft to talk with the captain.

At about two o'clock a faint breeze sprang up from the eastward. The sails gently filled, and there was the ripple of progress over the side of the boat. Soon the wind increased, and we made five knots an hour. By six o'clock it was blowing half a gale, dead ahead.

How proudly the *Nettie* dashed aside the waves, sending the white-caps high in the air, and landing them all over the deck! The water was of a deep, dark blue, and we sped along at a great rate. It was impossible, however, to lay our course for Seal Island, and so we concluded at ten o'clock to run for Portland, as we were in a pretty demoralized condition. The wind freshened still more, and the ocean seemed to be one mass of foam. The yacht heeled over to her work, and went like a magic creature. That was glorious sailing. We reached the city at about six P.M., and I have an impression that more gratitude was felt than expressed when we dropped anchor.

"It would be very pleasant," said Ruloff the next day, "instead of laying our course directly across to Seal Island, to work our way along quietly inshore until we reach Mount Desert, and then turn our face southward."

" Yes," I replied, "that would be better than the experience of the last two days. So long as we can just as well keep in smooth water we might as well do it."

And Bertric, "Although I enjoy being rocked in the cradle of the deep, and all that sort of thing, my impression is that a stationary bed once in a while is a healthy change."

And Stigand, " I must say that for a day or two at least I should like to keep within a reasonable distance of the land. The motion of the water didn't seriously affect me the other day, but still I should like to study the coast for a while."

And Algar, who is a perfect sailor, " I have just come across a man on shore who is a government pilot from Portland to Halifax, and who is ready to take our boat at an hour's notice."

So it was agreed to run for Mount Desert. Algar went ashore and made an arrangement with Edwards, who is thoroughly posted as to every reef and rock, and in a couple of hours the anchor was weighed once more, and we were gliding along among the islands of Casco Bay. Every one was in a gay mood that morning. We sang songs, told stories, and played practical jokes, as though we were all boys again. The breeze was from the southwest, and promised to hold all day. It was very gentle, to be sure, but with our three jibs and our two gaff-topsails we managed to work along at about six knots. At one time we found ourselves within a hundred yards of an island in water as smooth as a millpond; at another the *Nettie* rose and fell to the rhythmic will of the waters as we passed an opening between two sheltered spots. For hours we sailed thus, on this most perfect of all summer days, until at last we made Seguin, about twenty miles from Portland. The wind then began to freshen, and after consultation it was deemed a pity to lose such an opportunity to get across that much-to-be-dreaded Bay of Fundy, so we gave up our inshore plan, and laid our course E.S.E. directly for Seal Island. At one in the afternoon we were going at the rate of eight knots, and at two we crawled up to nine.

Such a day is very seldom met with. It was a white day in the journal of our trip, and the sailing was the very perfection of motion. That was yachting indeed. The sea was of that supernaturally deep blue, the sight of which seems to entirely satisfy a man, and fill him full, and make him feel that language is so poor a vehicle of exact expression that it is better to say nothing than to talk. We nevertheless kept saying to each other in an explosive sort of fashion, "Isn't it splendid!" "Isn't it magnificent!" and then, conscious that splendid and magnificent are very common words in which to describe such a sight, we fell to joining parts of words together, after the fashion of a friend of mine, and, marrying magnificent, after cutting away the last two syllables, to superb, after slicing off the first syllable, found some slight æsthetic satisfaction in calling the whole thing simply *magniperb.*

Such sailing as that was worship. I think my better nature is never more completely stirred than when I am gazing upon the broad deep, the most wonderful part of God's creation.

"God be with thee, gladsome Ocean!
  How gladly greet I thee once more!
  Ships, and waves, and ceaseless motion,
  And men rejoicing on thy shore.

"O, ye hopes that stir within me,
  Health comes with you from above!
God is with me, God is in me!
  I can not die, if Life be Love."

So sang Coleridge very sweetly, and so every heart
sings on such a glorious day as that. The grand ex-
panse was but the floor of a great cathedral, whose
groined roof was the over-arching heaven; and none
could stand within that sacred place and listen to the
great organ of the waters praising God without a bounding pulse and an ecstatic joy.

The sky was wondrously abysmal in its infinite depths
of color, and the few clouds, huge cumuli of snowy
white, shaded to a pearly gray in the middle, hung in
stately grandeur here and there, as though ordinary
clouds, like the rank and file of an army, had been left
in their encampment below the horizon, while the brig-
adier and major generals of vapor leisurely reconnoi-
tred the field of future action.

That livelong day we saw not a single vessel. We
were out of the beaten track of commerce; for the
fishermen, the lumbermen, and the steamers bound to
the east or west kept inshore. It was a very delicious sense of loneliness which filled our hearts with
wondrous satisfaction as we sped along. The land had
long since faded out of sight altogether, and the white-
caps were our only companions. The *Nettie* heeled
over to her work, and seemed to enjoy it as much as
any one. Every stitch of canvas told, for the wind

was on her quarter, and she hurried up to ten knots, as
though she were anxious to show her very best speed,
and brushed the water from her bow like a thing of
life. She would rise to the top of a wave, then, rushing down the other side, run her jib-boom into the next
wave, and afterward lift herself and shake the water
into spray. Hood has put this into better language
than I can command :

> " With quaking sails the little boat
>   Climbed up the foaming heap ;
> With quaking sails it paused awhile,
>   At balance on the steep ;
> Then, rushing down the nether slope,
>   Plunged with a dizzy sweep."

It was a kind of ecstatic pleasure to stand at her
bows and watch her as she plunged into a huge hill of
water, throwing it up on deck in a constant cascade.
And the musical rush of the waves along her side as
we lay on deck listening to it was a very delightful experience. The sound ceased almost altogether when
she lifted herself high in air, and then changed to a
grand chorus as she flung herself back into its bosom
almost up to her deck, with a grand swash which made
a bed of snowy foam all around her.

" What a difference there is, though, in the apparent
speed of vessels," I said to the pilot. " How fast are
we going, Edwards ?"

" Well," he answered, looking over the side, " about
six knot, I reckon."

" No more ?" I queried, disappointed.

" No, I guess not," was the answer.

The captain chuckled, and said in an undertone,
" Pshaw ! she's going ten, if she's going at all."

"Good," said Ruloff, "let's out with the log."

So we threw the log over, and in a quarter of an hour hauled it in again to find that she was trotting along at the rate of ten and a half knots.

"The pilot," said the captain, "has been accustomed to those blunt-headed coasters, which fight the water at every step, and make an awful bother when they travel; but our boat is as sharp as a knife, and goes right along without making any fuss about it."

About the middle of the afternoon the gentlemen were sitting by the cat-head, and I heard such a roar of laughter that I immediately went forward to have my part of the fun. They had been listening to a yarn which Fowler had reeled off, and the denouement was so incredible that they had greeted it with shouts of wild derision.

Fowler was a character. He was about sixty years of age, and a first-rate sailor; but he could tell the most preposterous stories about himself, and had just been indulging in this propensity.

"Well, you may laugh; but what I tell ye is the truth. I was there, and ought to know all about it. I wouldn't tell you what wan't true, and I don't make nothin' by tellin' it bigger'n 'tis."

"Come, come, Fowler; take off about fifty per cent., and we'll believe it," said Bertric.

"No, sir!" with a fearful emphasis on the sir; "I won't take off the worth of a spun yarn." And with that he began to chew vigorously on the mass of tobacco which filled his mouth.

"What is it, Fowler?" I said, as I joined the group.

"Yes, tell it again, and see what the dominie will

say. Tell it again; it's like a good sermon, and will
bear repetition."

"Oh, no," said Fowler, with a modest laugh; "I
don't tell no stories twice."

"Come, come, let's have it," I said, "and I will decide on its credibility."

So, with a kind of chuckle, he threw away the tobacco, fumbled in his pocket for a fresh supply, a sufficient quantity of which he cut off with a knife that
had seen hard service, and said apologetically—

"Well, I was only tellin' what actually happened to
me once;" and with that preface he shut the knife, put
the tobacco he had cut off into one side of his capa-
cious mouth, and began:

"You see, it was twenty-two year ago, and yet I remember it as if it was yesterday."

"Why, you said twenty years ago when you told it
to us," chimed in Stigand.

"No I didn't, neither; and if I did, what's two
years, I should like to know? Wall, whenever it happened, it was thus-wise, and what I'm goin' to tell ye
is as true as this wind's sou'west. I was on board the
schooner *Sarah Martin,* and it was the 9th of March,
and, more than that, it was at one o'clock in the morning. I tell you it was awful cold, though. The wind
whistled right through a feller's pea-jacket, and more'n
once I had to look down to see if I had forgot to put
any thing on when my watch was called—it was so
mighty freezing. Not much like this weather, I tell
ye; but a regular old Marcher, with snow and ice in
his teeth."

"Where were you, Fowler, and what were you
doing?"

"Where were I? why, we was off Nantucket, codding—that's where we was; and 'taint easy work pullin' in a fifteen-pound cod with a forty-fathom line, and findin' a dogfish on, either. Why, a feller's hands get so numb that he don't know he's got any, and thinks he's left 'em to home."

"Well, go ahead; what were you doing at one o'clock in the morning?"

"Doing? well, I'm just goin' to tell ye, only you won't let me tell a straight story. You get me all snarled up like a coil of wet rope, and it takes me a little while to get the kinks out, and tell it smooth."

"Good; take your own time, and if any man interrupts you again, we'll make him take an extra trick at the wheel."

"Wall, that would be a good joke. By Jiminy! ha, ha! where do you s'pose we'd go to if you should do that? I guess you'd have to put an extra watch on deck; and as for Halifax, well, we might drift there, and then agin we might not. Trick at the wheel! ha, ha! that would do well enough when we are at anchor; but Lord, such a day as to-day, if the skipper should tell one of you gents to keep her full and by, or to just give her a good full, and keep her skippin' along, you'd head her for Boone Island, like's not."

"Well, Fowler, uncoil your story, and I'll not interrupt you again."

"As I was a-sayin', we was coddin' off Nantucket; the wind blew heavy from the nor'east. There was a mighty sea runnin', and the cappen, seein' the rest o' the fleet had come to anchor, said to me, 'Fowler,' said he, 'hadn't we better let go our mud-hook?' I cast

my eyes to the norrard, and see it was goin' to blow
pretty stiff all night, so I said, 'You can do as you like,
Cap; but if she was my craft, I know what I'd do,
mighty quick.'

"'What's that?' sez he, kinder anxious; for I noticed he always come to me when it was a-blowing
hard.

"'Why,' sez I, 'them clouds, they look ugly, and it's
goin' to be a nasty night, and if we can get a fair hold
of the bottom, it's all right.'

" So the anchor was let go, and we bobbed about a
good deal worse than we did t'other night. That was
a mill-pond side of the sea we were in. Talk of
mountains—they war'n't nowhere side of them waves.
Why, sir, once the schooner pinted her bowsprit right
for the North Star, and you know she's got to stand
up pretty well on end to do that.

" I was just goin' out on the bowsprit to furl the jib,
when a flaw of wind took the sail, and at the same
minute a heavy wave struck us, and threw me off my
feet. I hung on to the clew of the jib, expectin' to be
landed against the larboard rail, you know. But the
wind was so strong it blew the jib outboard, and, instead of droppin' on the deck, I fell flat on my back in
the water. The tide was runnin' like a race-horse, and
when I got about midships, as I reckoned, a roller
lifted me about twenty feet above the deck, and I
hollered."

" You hollered?" said Bertric.

" Well, I guess I did, and the crew heard me, too,
and the cappen, he heard me. I struck out, hopin" to
get hold of the rail, but 'twar'n't no use. I give my-

self up for lost. No more coddin' for me, I said to myself. Just then I heard the cappen say—

"'I'm throwin' ye a line, Fowler,' and with that I heard a splash close to me. It was so dark I couldn't see nothin', but I heard the rope strike the water. I had the presence of mind to think that the rope would sink, so I fumbled round about a foot under water and caught hold of somethin'. It was the whippin' of the line.

"Well, I hung on with an awful grip, and could feel that they were haulin' away at t'other end. I never come so near faintin' in my life, but 'twar'n't no time to faint just then. The sailors was haulin' me on board, when one of them looked over the side and see that I had only the whippin' in my hand."

"I thought you said it was so dark you couldn't see," broke in Ruloff.

"Well, I was almost aboard then, and besides it lit up about two o'clock."

"Two o'clock," cried Stigand, "why, you fell off the bows at one. Were you in the water in March for an hour, and did it take you sixty minutes, with a strong tide, to go from the stem to the stern?"

"Wall, it might not have been exactly two, but it was nigh on to it; and besides that I was strugglin' all the time, and the time might have seemed a little longer than it really was; and more than that, I had to guess at the time, cos I couldn't let go that rope to get my watch out and see just the minute I was drownded," said Fowler, not in the least disconcerted.

"Well, when I was most up, one of the sailors, he

said, ' Cappen, hadn't we better get the gaff, and make fast to him ?' At that I must say I felt mad. It was bad enough to fall overboard, but to be gaffed as though I was a dogfish was more than I could stand, so I really believe I fainted away. At any rate the next thing I knew I was in the cabin stretched out on one of the transoms.

" The cappen stood over me, shaking me and saying, ' Fowler, let go that rope.' I looked down to my hand, and found that I had hold of about three inches of it, with such a grip that I couldn't let go. So I took hold of the rope with my right hand, and kinder coaxed it away from the fingers of the other hand.

" I tell you, that was a grip, though, wasn't it ?"

This remark was addressed to me, and I answered yes, without further comment on the adventure.

Just then we saw the captain hauling in the log, and to our delight we found that in the last four hours we had made a trifle over fifty miles. The wind still held its own, and the prospect for a speedy trip to Halifax was good.

That evening at sundown we feared the breeze would leave us, but, instead of beginning to die away at about four o'clock, and breathing its last at about seven, it held on until about nine, and died altogether at about twelve. For four hours we had a touch of the old experience. The stars shone brightly, the sky was clear and almost cloudless, but the swell was something awful for an inexperienced nervous system. Indeed, it is quite incredible that a vessel can roll as we did with not a breath of air stirring. The *Nettie* would be perfectly still for a moment, as though we were under a

lee, and then she would slowly heel over to the starboard, and continue to roll until she actually put her
rail under water, then straighten herself up, only to re-
verse the motion, and put her larboard rail under. The
accompanying diagram sufficiently accounts for any un-
pleasantness which may have arisen among the company on board. It is supposed to represent the lines
which a topmast would make against the sky, provided it were long enough to reach so far. I can scarcely look at it without discomfort. What sympathy,

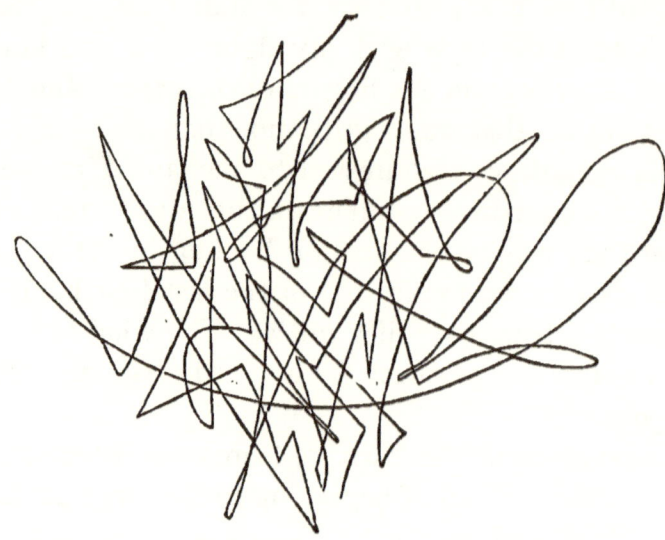

then, shall be given to one who experiences the sensations which in their fullness it so feebly suggests. The
huge mainsail was so ungovernable that we concluded
to take it in altogether. At two in the morning all
hands were called, and in about half an hour the canvas was snugly stowed, and the boom lashed as taut as
possible. I tried to sleep, but it was impossible. If I
lay on my back I found myself rolled like a barrel from

side to side of the berth. If I doubled myself up, and braced my knees against the side, I maintained my position until sleep relaxed my muscles, when I was rudely wakened with a vague impression that I was a huge lump of dough, and that a giant cook was kneading me. So I dressed myself, and spent the time until four in the morning on deck, when a breeze from the south steadied her, and I went below again, and was lulled to sleep by the music of the water playing against the side as we went through it. At seven we were going on at a spanking rate, and the day promised to rival the yesterday which we had enjoyed so much.

A good breakfast, and we were ready for any fate. Ah Boo, in whose presence we quote the favorite lines of Leigh Hunt, and say in chorus, "Abou Ben Adhem, may his tribe increase," until he breaks out into a fit of childlike laughter which lights up his dusky face with sunshine, prepared for us a very elaborate meal. We began our work with a luscious blue-fish, after which followed in quick succession mutton-chops, a tender steak, a morsel of salt meat, and what the sailors call slap-jacks of the most approved kind. A full man is always a hero ; the seat and source of prowess as well as good temper is the stomach. This is especially true on board ship.   •

At ten that morning we saw a fisherman on our lee bow, and determined to run him down, and find out exactly where we were. It is a pleasant experience to speak a vessel at sea. There is an excitement about it that breaks into the monotony of your life. We saw this schooner in the dimmest distance. She lay pretty nearly in our course. At first we could only discover the top of her main topmast. It was like a dull line against the sky. An unpracticed eye would never have detected it, but a sailor's eye is so trained to observation that nothing escapes it. In a little while we lifted the mast enough to see a few feet of the foremast, and after that we saw the rigging, and the masts coming apparently out of the water as though the hull were sunk, as indeed it was to our vision. By and by we saw the men on deck fishing. They had come from some point on the Nova Scotia coast, and could give us the information we wanted. We bowled along until we were within a hundred yards of her, when the captain cried, " Let her luff."

The wheel was put hard up, and in a minute more the sails were flapping.

" Ahoy there!" yelled the captain to those on the fisherman.

" Well, what is it ?" came back in answer.

" Which way are we from Seal Island?" said the captain, using his hands as a trumpet.

" East-southeast."

" How far ?"

" About thirty miles. Where are *you* from ?"

" From New York."

" Where bound ?"

" Gulf of St. Lawrence."

The jib was hauled to windward, the *Nettie* payed off slowly, and in a few minutes we were striking out at a wonderful gait. We sighted the light-house on Seal Island in an hour and a half, and then lay our course up the coast.

C

We were very fortunate in that we had no fog. We kept in sight of the land the rest of the day and all the next night. It was exciting to watch one light as it gradually faded to the size of a taper, and then went out altogether, and then to watch the darkness ahead until the dim taper twelve or fifteen miles farther on grew larger and larger until we got abreast of it, and counted it as another milestone passed. So the lights — some steady, some flash, some white, others colored—marked our path over the waters and told us just where we were.

I was up at twelve, for I was just a bit anxious, and at one o'clock thin gray streaks of light broke in the far east, and by two o'clock we could see quite well.

All along the Nova Scotia coast wrecks are to be seen. Schooners, lumbermen, full - rigged ships, and even ocean steamers are strewn on those merciless rocks. The day before we counted something like a dozen in the hundred miles we traveled.

There are very few buoys on this shore to mark the sunken reefs which threaten the life of every passing vessel, and the light-houses will in nowise compare with ours. The flash is not as brilliant, nor can it be seen at any great distance. One would think that on such a ragged coast every possible means of safety would be employed; but in these two important respects—lights and buoys, the almost sole dependence of the mariner in strange waters—the shore is strangely deficient.

No landsman can appreciate the feelings with which the sailor greets a light-house. Each one has its own peculiarity; and when a man peers into the black darkness and catches just the faintest possible glimpse of the light that burns in the headland tower, he feels like one who is getting into the midst of a group of friends. He watches it to learn whether it is a double or single flash, or whether it burns with a steady white blaze, and having determined that, he calls it by name, and knows where he is.

It is a part of our Christianity to look well to the light-houses along our shores.

> " The rocky ledge runs far into the sea,
>   And on its outer point, some miles away,
> The light-house lifts its massive masonry,
>   A pillar of fire by night, of cloud by day.

> "Not one alone ; from each projecting cape
>   And perilous reef along the ocean's verge,
> Starts into life a dim, gigantic shape,
>   Holding its lantern o'er the restless surge."

We sighted Sambro at about two o'clock in the morning. It is only six or seven miles from this light that the *Atlantic* went ashore. We had passed so many wrecks since we left Seal Island that we began to blame some one, we hardly knew whom, for not properly guarding a coast which seems to be the natural hiding-place of hurricanes, and a kind of trap for unwary vessels. It was on Blond Rock, S. $\frac{1}{2}°$ east, that the *Staffordshire* struck. Nearly all on board were lost, the number including the captain, who went down with his vessel. This dangerous spot ought to be buoyed and beaconed. The steamship *St. George* struck there about four years ago, and the only vessel the Cunard line has lost was lost on Seal Island. Farther on to the N.E. is Cape Niger, where a goodly vessel was bleaching her bones. It is a dangerous spot, not so much because of the ragged rocks which reach far out from shore, as because of the sunken reefs which a stranger who seeks shelter from the storm knows nothing about until he is on them. And so from the southwestern extremity to Halifax the whole Nova Scotia coast is a series of traps, with no sign-boards marked " Beware."

We kept at a respectful distance from Sambro, and entered the harbor of Halifax at four o'clock, making the run from Portland, including four hours of dead calm, in forty-four hours. This gave us an average of about eight and a half knots per hour, which we regarded as very fine sailing.

CHAPTER III.

BITS OF HISTORY.

"Any thing but history, for history must be false."—WALPOLIANA.

HE history of Nova Scotia is full of adventure and romance. While in Halifax I spent many a pleasant hour in recalling the appearance of the coast by which we had hurried so rapidly, and in posting myself up on the antecedents of a people who are, to say the least, pleasantly peculiar. It would be impossible to utter any thing but kindness of those who received us in the open arms of a generous and unstinted hospitality; and when we left the place it was with pleasant memories and many regrets. As is not unusual with cities, the traveler who lands at the wharf in Halifax gets a very unfavorable first impression. He enters upon dirty streets, lined with gin-shops, and all sorts of nameless snares for the honor and money of visitors. But when he ascends the hill, the residences are, many of them, palatial, and the view is superb. The bay lies at his feet, and stretches itself for miles toward the ocean. In the stream two men-of-war lie at anchor, while on the top of the hill are barracks for two regiments. These facts account sufficiently for the general feeling of demoralization with which one is oppressed. It is impossible to station any considerable detachment of an army near a city without producing injurious effects. Soldiers inevitably give a color to public opinion, and a general tone to society, which, with a subtlety all its own, detracts from the moral energy of the people.

I said to a gentleman who had been exceedingly kind to us, and who was thoughtful concerning these things, " Do you not find that these red-coats lower the mercury considerably?"

" Yes," he replied, without hesitation; "it is a great grief to many that the home government deems it necessary to keep such a force at this point."

" In what way does it affect you?" I queried.

" Well," he answered, " a soldier's life is at best a life of adventure. These gentlemen, I mean the officers, though they will compare favorably with soldiers the world over, are without the restraining influence of home-life. When a crowd of men get together, or live together, I do not care how high-toned they may be to start with, they become more or less reckless. They are in an abnormal condition; for men are not soldiers naturally—they are made soldiers by the stress of circumstances."

" And they are admitted into the best society?"

" Of course, many of them, if not all, have the right to demand it. Their social position, not reckoning their rank as our national defenders, makes us only too happy to open our doors and hearts to them."

" Well, how then do they hurt society?"

" I can hardly answer definitely, except by saying

that here, as in all garrison towns, what we call the
scarlet fever prevails to a large extent. Ladies are
always dazzled by military glory, and a red coat has
pretty much the same effect on them that it produces
on certain quadrupeds."

" How is it with the rank and file ?"

" Oh, they are a decided detriment. Two thousand
men, with nothing particular to do, and no moral re-
straints, will inevitably injure any community."

" But does not the presence of these soldiers and
sailors create a traffic which is of vital importance ?"

" Not so much as you would suppose. I believe
that, if the home government should see fit to remove
these regiments and these men-of-war, our trade, which
might suffer somewhat as an immediate consequence,
would find new channels, and the commercial importance of Halifax would be doubled in five years."

These sentiments express, so far as I can judge, the
feelings of many of the most thoughtful and patriotic
people of the city. War at best is barbarism, and it
is impossible to come in contact with it in any shape
without injury.

Halifax is curiously deficient in hotel accommodations. We put up at the Halifax Hotel, which by no
means answers to our definition of what a first-class
hotel ought to be. The city needs also a commodious public hall for various gatherings. We attended
an entertainment given by a popular reader in the best
hall in the city, where were congregated the *élite* of the
place, and were surprised to find it dingy and poorly
ventilated. The citizens of Halifax are very loyal to
their hillside home, and ought to see to it that a first-

class hotel and a worthy public hall are erected at once.
I do not say this with any desire to find fault, but simply in the spirit of friendly criticism. I give the impression made upon me in a city where I received at
the hands of many friends nothing but the most open-
handed hospitality, and, though I criticise as others
might in turn, though more sharply, criticise New
York, I bore away with me only the pleasantest memories, whose fragrance will abide.

One of the pleasantest and most amusing experiences of our sojourn in Halifax was connected with
Market-day. On Saturday morning of every week a
motley group, consisting of two or three hundred vend-
ers of all possible wares, take up their position around
and in the vicinity of the Province Building. Here
are to be found the most luscious wild strawberries, lying in the lap of huge leaves; fresh vegetables, arranged
in the most tempting way; early fruit, apples and mel-
ons, and all other articles necessary to a well-regulated
household.

In one corner sit a coterie of Acadians, who are said
to be so honest that they sleep with unbolted doors,
laboring under the impression that the rest of the
world is as simple as themselves. They are modest
folk, exceedingly timid, even to oppressive bashfulness;
coming to market among the earliest, and skittering
back to their homes the moment their wagons are
empty; never lingering to gaze into shop-windows, and
having little or no faith in the modern inventions
which make the farmer's life easy. They are deplora-
bly ignorant, hardly a dozen of them being able to
read or write. They are wonderfully exclusive, and

rarely marry out of their own class. It is curious that they are able to live within a few miles of such a place as Halifax without imbibing some of the notions with which the nineteenth-century brain teems. They avoid civilization, however, as though it were a pestilence, and come to town only to barter potatoes and turnips for flour and other absolute necessities.

Here in another corner is gathered a group of Indians. They are squalid to the last degree, and make a living by charging large prices for their woodenware. The old women sit glum and silent, vigorously weaving their twig baskets of many colors, while the more sprightly maidens, with swarthy faces and hair streaming down their backs, enter into a lively conversation about the merits of their goods. They are altogether a clumsy, dull-blooded set, apparently incapable of breathing the air of a city.

Yonder are the Negroes, than whom I have never seen either men or women more unsightly. The Indians exhibit the very perfection of neatness and thrift by the side of these helpless creatures. Darwin would delight in them as proofs positive of his pet theory. They are the missing link between the quadruped and the biped. Filthy beyond all expression, and incomparably lazy, they seem to be scarcely human. They come from a settlement a few miles from the other side of the bay, where they starve and freeze in the winter, and bask in the sun all summer. They are refugees from the slavery of the South, and have certainly not bettered their condition by taking up their abode on a foreign shore.

I said to a friend,

" Is there no work for them to do in such a place as this ?"

" Plenty," he replied, " but they won't do it."

" How do they get on, then ?"

" They don't get on at all. They just live, and no more. They did not rise when they escaped from the plantation, but fell to a worse estate, and there seems to be no help for them."

" But where do they live, and how ?"

" Well, you would scarcely call it living, if you saw them in their homes. They have a few huts, patched with mud, where they huddle, coming to town every Saturday to get a dime or two."

I noticed that they had few vegetables to sell. The girls had pailfuls of lilies, which they disposed of for a penny apiece, while the old women concocted a kind of root beer, which found its way down the œsophagus of the unwary once only, for I think the same person never drank twice.

I could not help thinking, however, that there is scarcely another place on the continent where two classes of people, like the Acadians and the Negroes, could live in proximity to, and in contact with, the busy life of a great city, without becoming amalgamated, and so far affected by its spirit as to lose such prominent peculiarities. If they lived within ten miles of New York or Boston, they would be trading jack-knives, swapping horses, and selling the real estate on which they had encamped, in less time than it takes to put a girdle around the earth, which, according to the most liberal estimate, is just forty minutes. The sweet Acadian damsels would preside over the households of thriving young men who had invaded their caste, and obliterated all lines of circumvallation, while the Negroes, taking shelter under the provisions of the Fifteenth Amendment, would send their children to school and run for Congress.

Nova Scotia presents a very varied and interesting history. It was probably discovered by those restless Cabots, a family consisting of a father and three sons, concerning whom the accepted records abound with the most delightful uncertainty. It is well proven, however, that they were daring sailors, setting the dangers of the sea at naught, and adding not a little to those romantic adventures which are the jewels of the fifteenth and sixteenth centuries.

Neither the birthplace nor the grave of the father is known. He is called a citizen of Venice, which right he won by a residence of something like fifteen years. He afterward took up his abode in Bristol, England, where he lived for years an uneasy sort of life, with his wife and three promising and stalwart boys. It was just about this time that public opinion began to change concerning the shape of the earth. People had been accustomed to think that they were living on a vast grassy plain, and firmly believed that if any one adventured to the edge, he would inevitably drop off and fall—somewhere or nowhere, geographers finding it difficult to determine which.

This new theory of sphericity assumed a practical shape at once. The European trade with the East Indies was of vast importance, and it was gravely concluded by the practical men of the day that, since it was such a fearful distance, sailing eastward, to the Indies, it must necessarily be a shorter distance sailing westward. That little notion changed the destiny of the race, and gave to six generations their character. It was, therefore, for purposes of trade that the first impulse was given by the well-to-do and ambitious merchants to these discoverers, who, within a century of the date above mentioned, made the world ring in praise of their prowess and their conquests.

Cabot had theorized himself into a state of great excitement, and fully made up his mind that a northwest course would certainly bring him to Japan and China. What is now known as the Sea of Sargossa, a vast tract of floating sea-weed, a sort of continental eddy, made it impossible to take a straight cut across the ocean. Once in these doldrums, one might lazily float for weeks and make no progress. Columbus sailed south of this region of calm, which is nearly as vast in extent as the Mediterranean, and Cabot determined to trust to luck on a northerly tack. The consequence was that Columbus effected a landing down by the Bahamas, while his rival came to anchor among the landslides of Labrador.

The successors of Columbus spent their efforts on the shores of the Gulf of Mexico, while those of Cabot laid claim to Newfoundland, Cape Breton, Nova Scotia, and the territory lying as far south and west as Nantucket.

On the fifth of March, 1496, John Cabot succeeded in getting a patent from the Seventh Henry, authorizing him to go where he pleased, steal whatever he might lay his hands on, and keep what he could. John

started with a single vessel, accompanied by his son
Sebastian, in May, 1497, to tempt his fate. The success of his expedition is told in the following quaint
letter from Pasquilizo to his brothers in Venice, and is
dated August 23d, 1497:

" The Venetian, our countryman, who went with a
ship from Bristol in quest of new islands, is returned,
and says that seven hundred leagues hence he discovered land, the territory of the Grand Cham. He coast-
ed three hundred leagues, and landed ; saw no human
beings. He was three months on the voyage, and on
his return saw two islands on his right hand, but would
not land, time being precious, and he was short of provisions. His name is Juan Cabot, and he is styled the
Great Admiral."

A year after this, in July, 1498, Don Pedro de Azala,
the Spanish embassador at the court of Henry VII.,
undoubtedly stirred to envy by the praise of Cabot's
exploits, which rang through London, wrote to Ferdi-
nand and Isabella a letter which in those hot-blooded
times might easily have been made a *casus belli.*

He said to their august majesties :

" I have seen the map which the discoverer has
made, who is another Genoese, like Columbus, and who
has been in Seville and in Lisbon asking assistance for
his discoveries. . . . I have seen on a chart the direction which he took, and the distance he sailed, and I
think that what he has found, or what he is in search
of, is what your majesties already possess."

Well spoken for an embassador who did not propose to have the glory of his native land dimmed by
the exploits of a rival explorer.

The name of the little craft in which the Cabots sailed was the *Matthew*. Where he sailed it is not easy to determine; but he must have gone far north, for, when on the starboard tack on his return trip, he saw Newfoundland on his right hand.

I do not much believe that the old gentleman ever landed on what is called Nova Scotia. His son Sebastian, however, in May, 1498, started with two ships from Bristol, and became so involved among icebergs that he steered for the south, and made a harbor on the mainland. This was undoubtedly the picturesque peninsula of which we are speaking.

Nova Scotia was first colonized by Des Monts and some Frenchmen, with a slight leaven of Jesuits, in 1604. They called that whole section of country Acadia. After this date the colonists became involved in endless quarrels among themselves and with the English, who, under a patent granted by James I., claimed the territory, and called it Nova Scotia, or New Scotland, which quarrels had no cessation until the Treaty of Paris, February, 1763, when France, tired out by the continual muss, surrendered all claim to the place.

Americans ought to be interested in this whole section of country, because it was once a part of our own domain, and because, if coming events cast their shadows before, it is very likely to become so again. When the old charter of Massachusetts was forfeited, and, under William and Mary, a new one was obtained, the colony of New Plymouth, the province of Maine, and Nova Scotia were all annexed to it. The only reservation made by the British government, I believe, was the right to cut timber any where in the forests suitable for masts for the Royal Navy.

The topography of Nova Scotia is exceedingly monotonous. The highest spot is Arthur's Seat, which rises only 810 feet above the sea, while the average height of the hills is not far from 500 feet. The soil on the southern coast is very thin indeed, and what on better land would be called agriculture, there reaches only the questionable dignity of scratchiculture. The inhabitants obtain a precarious living, and, though the hamlets and villages consisting of a few hundred inhabitants are numerous, there is scarcely a large-sized town, with the exception of Halifax, from Seal Island Light to White Head. One is saddened at sailing day after day for hundreds of miles along a coast which affords so few means of living. The people are almost universally fishermen, going out in their little boats a distance of nine or ten miles after cod, or setting their seines for herring in the harbors, or visiting their lobster-pots twice a day. These are their only sources of revenue. They live in the poorest and scantiest way, seldom acquiring the traditional penny which is taken from the stocking on a rainy day.

We were hardly surprised, when landing for the purpose of discovering how they lived, to find them exceedingly ignorant. Few newspapers ever reach those secluded spots, and few churches are to be seen. They live from hand to mouth, and seem to be content, not with little, but with what they can get.

We were struck, however, by the depth of water in the numerous harbors. Few places on the earth afford such shelter for vessels. Every few miles a splendid

lee invites the traveler who sees a storm coming.
And yet these are rendered dangerous of approach by
the lack of buoys to indicate the presence of sub-
merged rocks and reefs. The home government could
expend a few thousand pounds in no better way than
by erecting beacons and anchoring buoys along this
dangerous and treacherous coast, where unknown and
changing currents suck the unwary vessel to sure destruction.

I wonder that our own government has not made a
move in this direction. Our fishing fleet is so large
that the money which is lost in a single year by that
daring and too little appreciated part of our population which furnishes the world's Sunday breakfast-
table with its delicious compound of cod and potato
would suffice to put a warning hand on every rock
and on the edge of every channel along the entire
coast. The waters within a few miles of shore are a
regular highway along which thousands of vessels travel every winter. Between Halifax and the Gut of Canso
there are twenty-four commodious harbors, safe shelter-
ing-places from the "harricanes" which sometimes strike
a fleet with appalling suddenness; and at least ten out
of the twenty-four have a sufficient depth of water to
float ships of the line. Hardly one of them is properly buoyed, and the captain who is driven by stress of
weather or the loss of spars and sails in a gale to find
a lee, must do it at the risk of losing his craft.

This country could do nothing at the present time
more profitable or creditable to itself, and nothing that
would give it more popularity among those who are
compelled to sail these waters in December as well as

July, than the creation of a commission that would arrive at some understanding with the British government, and ultimate in planting, at the mouth of every harbor, a beacon on every rock that dares show its treacherous head above water, and anchoring buoys off every sunken reef along the whole coast of Nova Scotia. I have visited the fishermen who go from Gloucester and other points to the Gulf of St. Lawrence, and have found only dread of this shore. They universally heave a sigh of relief when they get by White Head. They are certainly a hardy and deserving race, encountering untold dangers every year, and have the right to claim at our hands all possible exemption from peril.

There is hardly a branch of industry in the world that is attended with such risk as our fisheries. When you watch the white sails of a fleet lying in the harbor, you get the impression that life on board such weatherly craft must be very pleasant, and you almost envy the favored fellows who have a good berth. But when they lie-to under try-sails on the Banks, or in a heavy gale part their hawsers, and tumble down on each other, the feeling of envy changes to pity. It is one thing to skim the summer sea, and quite another to brave the snowy blast with the mercury cuddling about zero to keep warm.

During the last forty-three years Gloucester alone has lost fourteen hundred and thirty-seven men, and two hundred and ninety-six vessels. This makes the fearful average of thirty-four lives and seven vessels yearly. It is impossible to run over this long catalogue of disasters, remembering that every winter adds to it, without a feeling of admiration for the rough but hardy and heroic fellows who brave death every time they weigh anchor. If it is possible to encourage them amid their perils, it should be done; and if by the expenditure of a comparatively paltry sum we can assist them to successfully defy the storm, we ought not to be laggard in coming to their aid.

I have lately come across a narrative in a little book called " The Fisherman's Memorial and Record Book," published in Gloucester, which puts the constant perils of our brave sailors in such vivid light that I reproduce it without apology. It is the recital of a very common experience, only in too many instances the issue is fatal. No one can read it without a feeling of sympathy for those who bid their wives and children farewell with a strange feeling that the chances are against their ever seeing them again.

"The winter of 1862 found me out of employment, and I determined to gratify my long pent-up inclination of going to Georges. It was early in February. The weather had been extremely mild for the season, and there were busy times at the wharves in Gloucester.

"Upon going to the fitting-out store of Messrs. ———, I was cordially received. They were surprised to learn that I wanted to go to Georges, and endeavored to dissuade me from my purpose. Their persuasions were of no avail, however; and, as they had a vessel which would be ready to sail in a day or two, they told me I could have a chance in her. Procuring the necessary additions to my outfit, I entered heartily into the work of getting our craft in readiness. The ice-house in the hold was filled with the crystal blocks, the cable and anchors overhauled, gurry-pens placed in position, bait of fresh herring packed in the ice, provisions taken care of, and the vessel put in a taut and strong condition.

"On the morning of February 14th we started, and, in a glorious run of twenty-four hours, sighted the fleet on the Banks—nearly a hundred sail, riding at their anchors, half a mile, and, in some instances, a mile apart. It was a pretty sight, and the fine, clear weather rendered it highly enjoyable. We could distinctly see the men at the rail pulling in fish, rapidly as hands and arms could move. Soon our position was selected, the anchor was down, and the crew were busy getting ready to try their luck.

"The cold, to one of my constitution, was intense, and pierced into the very marrow of my bones, although I was thickly clothed. But this deep-sea fishing was so exciting that I stood at the rail sometimes a full hour, without changing my position, pulling in the big cod-fish, and occasionally a halibut. It was a moment of supreme gratification when I hauled in my first fish of the latter species, and saw him floating alongside with the hook securely fastened in his mouth. One of the crew helped me to gaff him over the rail, and I felt myself master of the situation. Our steward, a Portuguese, was a clever fellow, and, in honor of my first halibut, brought me a mugful of hot coffee, and a pancake with plums in it, called by the fishermen a 'joe-flogger.' Pulling in these big fish from so many fathoms down, against a strong tide, was work I was not accustomed to, and glad enough was I, after partaking of a hearty supper, to turn into my bunk, and be lulled to sleep by the tossing of the billows.

"The crew were a jolly set, and for several days the weather was fine, the fish abundant, and the fun immense. We had changed our berth twice, each time drawing nearer to the body of the fleet, and each time finding the fish more plentiful. I began to think that the Georges fishery, after all, was not so bad as it had been represented, although it used to fret me exceedingly to see so many of the vessels lying so near together, knowing full well that in case of a sudden storm and they dragged their anchors, or chafed off their cables and went adrift, collision would be inevitable. But there being no apparent danger, I dismissed the thought in keeping busy.

"We now had more than half a fare, and the skipper remarked, one afternoon, as he lit his pipe,

"'Boys, if our luck holds on, by another week we'll think of putting our craft on the homeward tack.'

"This was cheering, and we finished up the day with a good catch. At sundown there was quite a sudden change in the weather. The clouds massed, and the rising wind made the sea rough. All signs indicated an approaching storm. It was a wild-looking night; the vessels tossed up and down like cockle-shells. At eight o'clock the skipper began to get uneasy. He kept looking up at the sky, and then glancing along the horizon. Ben, my chum, whispered to me,

"'Depend on it, we're going to have a tough one out of this; and I shouldn't wonder if you had a chance to see more o' Georges than you'll ever want to see ag'in. I've been with the old.man half a dozen years, and when I see him walkin' and lookin' that way, I make up my mind that som'thin's goin' to happen.'

" By this time the sky had grown inky black, the wind had veered to the northeast, and was increasing in violence. It began to snow—moderately at first, then more fiercely fell the white flakes. The skipper went forward and examined the cable, then gave orders to pay out some ten fathoms or more, which was done. Our lights in the rigging had been lit since sundown, and all about us were the lights of the fleet, looking so prettily as they danced up and down with the motion of the vessels. The skipper, upon being asked what he thought, replied :

" ' We'll have a tough time 'tween now and morning, and the watch must keep a sharp lookout for drifting vessels. If the rest of you want to take a nap, do it now, as there won't be much sleeping a couple of hours from now.'

" All hands except the watch went below at about half-past eight o'clock. I could not remain there, but kept going on deck. It was something new and terrible to me, and, as I was well wrapped, I did not suffer much from the wet and cold. But I did feel anxious, and would have given all I possessed to be safely at home. But wishing was of no avail —here I was, and I must take my chance with the rest. We can die but once, thought I, and I began to have serious thoughts. Not that I was afraid of death—no, that was not the feeling ; but there was one at home whom I wanted to see, and, holding her hand in mine, I should have been better reconciled. But perhaps it is as well not to tell all my thoughts at that fearful time. We have singular fancies in hours of danger.

" It was now about eleven o'clock. The wind had risen fearfully, the snow came down spitefully, and the sea rose higher than I had ever supposed it possible for it to rise, and was covered with snowy caps of foam. The sensation of being tossed up and down so violently, together with the darkness and the storm, were not pleasing, and it seemed to me that every plunge the vessel made would be her last.

" As midnight drew near the gale increased fearfully. I had never experienced any thing so terrific before, and the stories which had been told on board the mackerel-catcher now assumed a more truthful aspect. How the winds shrieked through the cordage, and the waves leaped, seemingly impatient to add us to the many victims which have been swallowed up on this treacherous spot ! My shipmates showed no signs of fear ; they were all on deck, and the skipper was keeping a sharp lookout. Ben was also on the alert, and had placed a hatchet near the windlass, to be in readiness should it be deemed necessary to cut our cable. As he came near where I was standing, he very coolly remarked 'that if we did not break adrift ourselves, or some other vessel didn't run into us, he thought we might ride it out.' To me it seemed an utter impossibility for any vessel to stand such a gale; but I said nothing. The great danger to be apprehended was from collision, as in case either ourselves or some other of the fleet lost their anchor or parted their cable, away they would go with fearful speed; then, if they struck another craft, good-bye to both of them—there was not the slightest hope for either.

"The darkness was impenetrable, and a more dismal night I never passed. How I longed for morning to dawn! Once in a while the storm would lull for a little time, then we could see some of the lights of the fleet; but this was not often. We knew the situation ere the storm came on, but now we must wait till daylight. The hours dragged heavily along —anxious hours they were. They are indelibly impressed on my memory, and will not be effaced until death claims me. During the night a large vessel passed quite near us. We could see her lights, also her spars and sails, as she sped swiftly along on the wings of the storm. Glad enough were we to have her pass us, and I trembled at the thought of our fate had she struck our little craft. When I learned the terrible disaster of the gale, I came to the conclusion that this vessel was the cause of some portion of it.

"At length the east began to lighten; morning was coming. What a relief it was when the day dawned! Our danger was not over, for the gale still continued, but there was a comfort which the light brought that did me good. The fearful darkness of the night and that terrible uncertainty were relieved, as we could now see our position and better guard against the threatening dangers. Our vigilance was not relaxed. We had something to eat, and then kept up our watching, for the storm still continued its fury. Somewhere about nine o'clock the skipper sang out, 'There's a vessel adrift right ahead of us! stand by with your hatchet, but don't cut till you hear the word!'

"Ben was there at his post. He could be trusted at such a time, and would await orders—this all on board knew full well. All eyes were now bent on the drifting craft. On she came! It was a fearful moment to me, and it was evident that the men—some of whom had followed Georges fishing for ten seasons—thought there was danger now, but they were not afraid. There they stood, determined to do their best for their lives. I knew I should share the same fate with them, and there was some consolation even in this. The drifting vessel was coming directly for us; a moment more, and the signal to cut must be given! With the swiftness of a gull she passed by, so near that I could have leaped aboard, just clearing us, and we were saved from that danger, thank God! The hopeless, terror-stricken faces of the crew we saw but a moment, as they went on to certain death. We watched the doomed craft as she sped on her course. She struck one of the fleet a short distance astern, and we saw the waters close over both vessels almost instantly, for as we gazed they both disappeared. Then we knew that two vessels of the fleet would never again return to port.

"We had little time to think of others, as we began to drag our anchor, and yaw about too much for safety. This was dangerous in the extreme, for if the anchors did not take hold again we must cut our cables, and, once adrift, we knew our fate. Fortunately, the anchors found holding-ground, and we rode again in safety.

"All through the day we watched. Twice was our safety endangered by vessels adrift, but they went clear. We were saved! At sundown the gale moderated, but we knew that many a poor fellow who had left Gloucester full of hope would never more return; that many a wife would never again see her husband, and mothers and brothers and sisters would have cause to remember the terrible gale which had swept so fearfully over the Georges.

"I was on nettles all next day, as I thought the skipper would immediately start for home. But judge of my surprise to see the men coolly get their lines in readiness for fishing, just as though there had been no storm, no danger or peril but a few hours ago. This was indeed intensely practical. They smoked and talked of getting a fare with so much coolness that it really seemed terrible to me. 'Supposing we should catch another gale—what then?' I received for a reply that 'they had come to get a trip of fish; I, to see how I liked Georges.' We fished through the week, had good luck, and it was a happy moment when the skipper said, 'Get the anchor; we'll turn her nose homeward.' Eastern Point Light, when first sighted, looked cheering and friendly. As we passed in by the Fort, there was a crowd of people, and as they saw our vessel's name there was rejoicing. Several came on board, asking if we had seen such or such a vessel since the gale. The town was in commotion. Such anxiety I hope never again to witness.

"When the vessel came alongside the wharf, I put my luggage out, and concluded not to repeat the experiment of making a trip to Georges in midwinter. When I got home, they told me I had grown much older in the few weeks of my absence. What I experienced during that night and day of storm was enough to make any one, especially a green hand, grow old. I have no desire to try it again. If the reader wishes a similar experience, perhaps it would be well for him to take a trip, but I advise all such to make their wills ere they leave port."

Barry Cornwall has beautifully framed the facts in these striking lines:

" A perilous life, and sad as life may be,
  Hath the lone fisher on the lonely sea,
  O'er the wide waters lab'ring, far from home,
  For some bleak pittance e'er compelled to roam;
  Few hearts to cheer him through his dangerous life,
  And none to aid him in the stormy strife;
  Companion of the sea and silent air,
  The lonely fisher thus must ever fare;
  Without the comfort, hope—with scarce a friend,
  He looks through life, and only sees—its end."

CHAPTER IV.

AMONG THE ROCKS IN A FOG.

"The mist that like a dim soft pall was lying,
  Mingling the gray sea with the low gray sky."
  HIGGINSON.

"Thus, while to right and left destruction lies,
  Between the extremes the daring vessel flies,
  But haply she escapes the dreadful strand,
  Though scarce her length in distance from the land."
  FALCONER.

E started from Halifax on Saturday morning at about half-past eleven. There was just a breath of air, enough to tempt us out into deep water; but when we were to the eastward of Sambro it left us to drift with the tide. By this time, however, we had learned to take matters very philosophically, and not chafe at any fate which might beset us. A man who has not become used to the freaks of the ocean, and who can not take its whims and caprices as so many jokes to be laughed at, feels like a chained lion when he is on the water in a dead calm. It is a great shock to the nervous system to know that you are within a few miles of land, and yet too far off to think of rowing the distance, and to gaze on the spires and cupolas of the neighboring city which invites you to pleasures you can not enjoy.

If it has ever been your misfortune to lie down in a very narrow berth in a steamboat, amid pitchy and tangible darkness, and to allow your imagination to work until you felt as though you were in a coffin, the lid of which was being screwed down by invisible hands, and the air of which was being gradually exhausted, you can get some faint idea of the misery of being becalmed off soundings, but within sight of land, when one is in a hurry to reach his destination. The days were wearing away, and we had already left a couple of weeks of vacation behind us; and it did seem hard to be drifting a few miles up the bay with the flood, and then a few miles out to sea with the ebb tide, when we wanted so much to be chasing the deer in Newfoundland or catching salmon on the coast of Labrador. Still, it is necessary for a yachtsman to possess his soul in patience, and to take gratefully whatever the winds and waters choose to give him. He must be ready and willing to go when and where he can, not when and where he would like to.

Ah Boo is a fisherman. How he spent his dusky youth I know not, but shrewdly suspect that he coaxed the finny tribe of his native waters with the universal pin-hook. He poked his head up above the gangway, and with an explosive " Oh! no wind! me fish and have chowder for dinner," made a raid on the cockpit for a line, which he captured and carried triumphantly to the fore-rigging. He handled the fresh clams, which had been purchased for just such an emergency, with a tender care, as though each one contained a pearl, and

D

at last selected two or three overgrown and plethoric bivalves as a tempting bait.

"Ah Boo, you propose to feed the fish well," I said, as the three luscious morsels dangled from his hook in delightful confusion.

"Yes, yes," he replied, "me feed 'em well, then they feed us well;" and with that he threw the three-pound sinker with a deft cunning which proved that he was no apprentice.

The line ran out ten, twenty fathoms, when I said, "Why, steward, there's no bottom."

"Oh yes, me find bottom soon," replied the cheery fellow as he patiently uncoiled more line, and was rewarded by feeling the lead touch the sand below. He took his seat on the rail, and with his right hand drew the line up a foot or two, then let it fall back again, after the most approved fashion.

"Now come on, fish, and bite my hook. I want you; I want chowder; come on," he said, as though holding converse with the inhabitants below. Just then came a twitch. He was on his feet in an instant, and hauling in the line hand over hand. When he had recovered about half of it, he stopped to catch breath and assure himself that the fish was on, when, with a very expressive "Oh, he gone; he no bite good," he dropped the line down again, and waited patiently for number two.

In a few minutes I heard him again conversing with an invisible somebody, and tugging away at his line, as though there were a whale at the end of it.

"Me got him this time; big fellow, too." And then addressing his remarks to the fish, "Only little way more, Mr. Cod; keep hold good, and I have you safe on deck."

With that he pulled very steadily, and soon landed a fine haddock, weighing about ten pounds.

"I got you now, ole feller," he said, as he took him by the gills and hauled the hook out. "Look, Mr. Hepper; big fish, big chowder," and he chuckled.

He hurried below for his knife, and began his work by remarking, "No let fish die—kill him ; more quicker kill him, more better eat," and with that he gave the fish a blow on the head which would have stunned a bullock.

"Now, then," said the captain, coming upon the scene of action, "I'll make a chowder myself. You can beat me all holler in preaching, Mr. Hepworth, but I don't give in to any one in making chowder. Steward, give me that knife."

Ah Boo is accustomed to obey, and so reluctantly gave the knife to the captain, and sought his retreat below, saying to himself, "Me make good chowder too. Me no sail vessel, but me make chowder more better'n cappen."

The captain handled that haddock in the most masterly and yet in the tenderest way. With a cut just forward of the pectoral fins, he got at the root of the gills, which he removed as skillfully as a first-class surgeon would perform a brilliant operation. He then turned the fish over on his side, and made a slit down the back on either side of the dorsal fins, which seemed to come out of their own accord. He performed the same operation on the anal fins, and then, cutting the haddock open, removed the entire spinal column. He handled the head also in a way not easily described, but which resulted in the removal of about half, while the other half was strung on the body like a huge bead, and the work was done.

"There," said he; "I want some pork, some hard bread, and some toast, and I'll show you a dish fit for a king."

Let me skip over the rest of the morning, for I am so interested in the chowder that I would fain linger in the vicinity of the cook-room until the grand finale. The fragrance of that most mysterious and most delicious combination hovers about my memory still, and no one was backward when, at one o'clock, Ah Boo called out,

"Dinner ready, sir."

"Now, then, captain, you are on trial," cried Bertric, as he received what would have sufficed for most men, but what proved to be only the introduction to a hearty dinner.

"All right," he replied, with a chuckle, as though he were sure of the victory.

We tasted, and with loud acclamations cheered the captain. The innumerable ingredients had been mixed with such cunning that nothing was wanting, except perhaps more chowder.

The calm hung on with a grip like that with which Fowler held to the rope, all that afternoon and during the entire night. We spent the time until ten o'clock in the discussion of subjects grave and gay, in looking over the slender stock of literature which our yacht library contained, and in games of draughts, and then went to bed.

I may say just here that our enthusiasm concerning taking our trick at the wheel and our watch at night gradually faded until it was lost to sight, though it remained to memory dear. We felt, you know, that it might destroy the discipline necessary on a cruise of that kind to interfere with any of the duties of the crew. Besides, we noticed that the captain made up his slate without any reference whatever to us, setting his regular watches from the forecastle, and then came to ask how we proposed to pass the night. We felt the slight, because of the implied want of confidence in our ability, which was perhaps justified by the fact that every one of us had been found more than once fast asleep at his post. One evening the captain came on his customary errand, and said,

" Mr. Hepworth, where will you watch to-night?"

I replied, " Well, Cap, if it makes no difference to you, I will take my watch in my state-room, from ten o'clock until about six in the morning."

The captain saw that the knotty problem was solved at last, and chuckled as though he had anticipated just that result. However, he put a grave face on the matter, and turning to Ruloff, said,

" Mr. Ruloff, which is your watch?"

Ruloff replied, with great dignity, as though the fate of the voyage was to be decided by his action,

"Cap, after due deliberation, I have concluded to take a sort of dog-watch from four to six in the afternoon."

"And you, gentlemen?" he continued, turning to Bertric and Stigand.

"Well," said Bertric, looking at a huge English terrier we had with us, "if Ruloff takes the dog-watch, Stigand and I will watch the dog."

But Algar still clung to his duty. He really liked to sit up at night and look out for light-houses, and be ready in case of a tack or a change of wind, or any other emergency.

And so ended, most ignominiously, our experiment of the Corinthian method of yachting. It is very delightful in theory to take control of your own vessel, and to become part and parcel of the work done; but in practice it is not pleasant to be shaken out of a warm sleep on a rainy midnight, with a gruff "Come, come, our watch is up."

You ask the intruder, "How is the weather, John?"

"Raining hard, sir."

"And the wind?"

"Nor'-east, and blowing a gale."

You reluctantly rub your eyes, then crawl into your clothes, pull on your rubber boots, get into your rubber coat and hat, and grope your way on deck, to find it dark as the inside of a tar-barrel, while the vessel is pitching and rolling at a fearful rate. The Corinthian method is very good in a harbor, and it is not exactly irksome if it consists in giving orders to your sailing-master to go from one port to another, and to govern himself accordingly, after which piece of advice you retire to the passenger list, and take life easily. I confess to a constitutional make-up which renders it impossible for me to thoroughly enjoy taking my share of the detailed drudgery of sailing. I like to sleep when ten o'clock comes, though I am not greatly averse to taking my watch from nine to twelve; but deliver me from standing at the cat-head on a drizzly night from twelve to four. I really do not like it. Up to midnight, time seems to wag along at a reasonable rate; but after that it seems as though the old fellow, with a feeling that most every body was asleep, and would not discover his lapse, lay down once in a while and took a nap himself.

Late on Sunday morning a gentle breeze broke the monotony of our life, and we found ourselves gliding along at about six knots an hour. The afternoon was lovely—

> "So calm, so cool, so bright,
> Bridal of earth and sky;"

and the scene around us was well fitted to excite a thoughtful soul to worship. It required no great stretch of the imagination to make us feel that we were in a vast temple, in which no uttered sermon was necessary, since the whole scene preached to us with an eloquence not to be equaled by the most persuasive periods. The roof of this vast temple was the arched sky, with its background of unutterably deep blue. It was frescoed by the ever-changing clouds, with their neutral tints. The hills on shore, and the lofty and rugged mountains in the dim distance, seemed like giant pillars, while for music we listened to the rippling waters as our sharp bow cut through them. We sat together on the forward deck, watching the land as it sped by us like the unfolding of a panorama, and sang hymns in which the sailors joined—for we had a very remarkable crew — and then bowed ourselves in prayer to Him who holdeth the waters in the hollow of his hand. There is a Sunday on the sea as

well as on the land, a kind of unwonted calm, which
disposes to thoughtfulness.

Only one thing tempted us. The birds—loons, ducks,
and gulls—seemed to be aware of the character of those
on board, and with a defiant kind of persistency settled
within easy range. It was almost too much for Fletch.
He saw half a dozen sea-pigeons on the larboard bow,
and felt constrained to put his hands in his pockets
and clinch his fists, lest he might be tempted to shoot.
"Oh, if it were only Monday morning!" he exclaimed,
as a flock lit on the water close to us, "wouldn't I
make you suffer, though!" And once the opportunity
was more than he could bear. He rushed into the
cabin, got his double-barreled gun, and was about to
draw a fatal bead, when he checked himself, evidently
with a mighty effort, and carried his weapon back,
muttering, "No, I won't shoot to-day; but if you show
your heads to-morrow, woe be unto you—that's all I
say."

On Monday came an experience which all on board
will remember. We suffered a very narrow escape,
and withal came so near to a disastrous end of our
trip that we shall never cease to be thankful. It happened in this wise.

At about two o'clock in the morning I was roused
from a deep sleep by the sharp cry—

"Let her come about!"

In an instant I was out of bed, and my clothes, as
though they appreciated the situation, seemed to put
themselves on me. I do not believe I was more than
two minutes dressing. I groped my way through
the cabin, and was soon on deck. The dull gray

streaks of morning were tingeing the eastern horizon, and we could see perhaps a quarter of a mile ahead.

" What's the matter, Captain ?" I said, as I saw Comstock, who was evidently in an unusual mood.

" Rocks ahead, sir," he replied, somewhat sharply.

I went forward, and saw, about one hundred yards off, a reef of hungry-looking rocks, toward which we had been directly heading, and on which we should have inevitably run had it been an hour earlier. The yacht lay too, her sails shivering in the wind, while we took in the situation, and made up our minds what it was best to do.

" How came we here ?" I asked the pilot, who at that moment appeared on deck with the most disorderly toilet, one shoe off, and only one arm in the sleeve of his pea-jacket.

" Why, we kept close inshore all day yesterday, and, though I shot her out into open water at night, the current has sucked us right back again among the rocks—that's what's the trouble. The truth is, this is a nasty coast ; there ought to be no night here at all, for it's not easy getting clear of these reefs even in the daytime."

" Well, Cap, what shall we do ?"

" The pilot must decide that question," he replied. " These are not Christian waters, and I don't know any thing about them. If I were only in a civilized place, now, I'd know where I was, but when a man gets down here, he gets beyond the reach of the Christian religion."

Just then the pilot, Edwards, came up to me, and said,

"What shall we do, Mr. Hepworth—go on, or run in? Country Harbor lies just to the norrard, and we can make a lee in the course of an hour or so. Just look there."

I turned in the direction indicated, and saw to the southwest a huge bank of fog, which was coming toward us rapidly, and in a little while would probably shut us in completely. We were hedged in by reefs, some just above water, and others just below, their positions indicated only by the white-caps above them. I said to Edwards,

"Well, we want to get on as fast as possible. Even if the fog comes in, we are safe enough if we get eight or ten miles out; and it ought not to be difficult to lay our course for the little Gut of Canso."

"All right, sir," he replied, and the *Nettie* was headed for open water. We bowled along for a while, when it was suggested by some one that it would only take us five or six hours to get to Whitehead, while the fog might last for three days; that when opposite Whitehead we should have to feel our way in, as we could not keep on our course; that we wanted to get into the Gulf of St. Lawrence as soon as possible, and there was no use in running a hundred miles to the eastward of it. The prospect of spending three or four days in the fog outside of the Roaring Bull was not very inspiring, and so I countermanded my order, and the yacht was put about. The man at the wheel had no sooner got his helm hard down than the fog came driving in like magic, and Edwards had just time to note the positions of the several rocks at the mouth of Country Harbor before all about us was thick, impenetrable darkness. I have been in fog many a time, but in none like that. It was impossible to see the length of the vessel. The moisture gathered and stood on our pea-jackets in large drops, keeping my eye-glasses so moist that I was compelled to take them off, which was well-nigh equivalent to being blind.

There was a heavy swell on, but the wind was not too strong. Edwards had caught sight of the two principal reefs about half a mile ahead, and it was a great relief to us all when after sailing for fifteen minutes we felt sure that we had passed them. Every man was on the forward deck except Fowler, who had the wheel. ·

By and by the swell ceased, and we were in still water. We knew by that that we had passed to the northward of the headland, and were somewhere inside the harbor.

" John, heave the lead," said the captain.

Little John, as we called him, stood at the main-rigging, line in hand, while Big John took the end of the line with the lead·attached forward, and, giving it a swing, hurled it twenty feet ahead.

"Fifteen fathom, and no bottom!" was the first cry.

"Good! Safe so long as we are in that depth of water, unless the rocks bring us up."

"There ain't no rocks here," said Edwards. "We can't run into any thing except the beach. I want to get over on the other side, if possible, because there's good holding-ground there. We must be mighty near the norrard shore."

"Ten fathoms!" shouted John.

" Now, then, look out ahead there, and see if you can find land. One of you fellows crawl out on the jib-boom, and keep your eyes peeled."

" Eight fathoms, shoaling!"

" That's so, and shoaling altogether too fast."   ·

" Breakers right ahead!" cried the man on the jib-boom, and at that moment John yelled—

" Four fathom!"

" Down with your helm," shouted the captain, and the *Nettie*, not lost yet, spun round as on a pivot.

Now, then, for the other tack. We were certainly inside the harbor, the water was so smooth, and it ought not to be very difficult to make the farther shore, where we could drop anchor in safety. ·

" Seven fathom!"

The water was deepening, and we felt relieved. Even the dog seemed to be conscious of a sense of security, for he wagged his tail at John when he announced the depth of water.

" Ten fathom!"

" Twelve fathom, and no bottom!"

" Now, then, we must grope our way in this thick darkness to the other side."

We sailed on for a while, when the order was given to slow her as much as possible. Fowler brought her up close to the wind, so that her sails began to flutter, and we forged ahead at a very modest rate.

" Heave the lead again!" ordered the captain.

" Nine fathom!" was the first piece of news.

" Look out sharp, out there on the jib-boom!"

" Aye, aye, sir!" came back the reply.

" Eight fathom!"

Shoaling again. We were all huddled together near the fore-rigging—one with a single boot on, another without hat, another in his shirt sleeves—peering into the fog to catch a glimpse of land.

" Seven fathom !"

" Edwards, there's an iceberg right ahead of us," I said to the pilot.

" No, it isn't," answered Ruloff, " it's a three-story house."

Whatever it was, it was close to us.

" Hard alee !" yelled the captain ; "here's the land right aboard of us."

" Down with the anchor !"

The *Nettie* shook her canvas in the wind again, the chain rattled through the hawse-holes, and in a minute more we were riding safely at anchor.

I noticed one peculiarity in every gentleman on board, which showed itself immediately after the anchor dropped.

Bertric went up to Stigand, and said confidentially— " Do you know, Stigand, I think Hepworth was afraid. Now I was a good deal excited, but I never felt freer from fear in my life, myself."

And Stigand went up to Ruloff, and in the same confidential whisper repeated the sentence concerning Algar, almost word for word.

And Ruloff repeated it to Algar concerning Bertric, and so on, until each had defended his own prowess in solemn whisper to every member of the company.

The truth is we were all scared nearly out of our wits. No man who has the common North American nervous organization, can go through such an experience as that without feeling very decidedly frightened. For myself, I am willing to confess here, though I did not do it at the time, that for an hour and a half I was listening to hear the deep "thud" of the *Nettie* on the rocks. I fully expected to lose the boat, and would have willingly compromised with Fate for the safety of the party.

I said to Edwards,

" Come, weren't you scared ?"

He looked at me in a blank sort of way, and replied,

" Skeered ? No ; but I was afraid we might tetch something comin' in."

" That's what I was afraid of, and that's what I call being scared," I thought to myself, as I went aft.

In about an hour the fog lifted, and we saw what might have happened. What I thought an iceberg proved to be a huge boulder about fifteen or twenty feet square, which the fog had magnified. It was in just the position to save us. But for it we should have gone plump on the beach. As it was, we were so near that you could almost lower yourself from the end of the jibboom to the land. It was on the whole about as narrow an escape as I care to experience, and I regard it as one of those episodes which are well enough to look back upon, but which it is by no means agreeable to pass through.

CHAPTER V.

TROUT AND MOSQUITOES.

"Among the plagues on earth which God has sent,
Of lighter torment, is the plague of flies.
Where wild America in vastness lies,
There diverse hordes the swamps and woods infest;
Banded or singly, there make man their prize."

BISHOP OF QUEBEC.

EFORE we started from Halifax we engaged the services of a regular hunter. He was a character worthy of study. He was already something over sixty years of age, and as hale and hearty as possible. He told me the story of his life one evening as we were sitting together; but I afterward found him to be such an egregious manufacturer of facts that my former admiration somewhat subsided. He brought all his tents and camp utensils on board, and promised us rare fishing and hunting when we reached the woods—promises, however, which were by no means fulfilled.

We found Country Harbor such a delightful place that we determined to remain in that region for a few days, and find out what sport was to be had. Its northern branch, a creek three miles long, is called Isaac's Harbor, and as this afforded a splendid lee

against almost any wind, we brought the *Nettie* to anchor in five fathoms, just off the little village on its
western shore.

Being in immediate want of provisions, I started out
on a foraging expedition, and soon came across a fisherman who had just harvested from his pots a load of
lobsters.

"Halloo, friend," I hailed, "will you let me have
some of your freight?" He rowed alongside, and I
picked out a dozen fine green fellows, who had just
come out of the water, and had not yet got over their
surprise at the new condition of things.

"How much apiece?"

"Well, I reckon that generally they are worth about
a penny apiece, but them dozen you can have for ten
cents."

I paid him the silver, and then his conscience seemed
to smite him for charging me an exorbitant price, for
he immediately picked out an immense lobster and
added it to the twelve that were kicking and tearing
each other in the bottom of the boat.

This is certainly a paradise of cheap provisions, I
thought, as we rowed to land. However, it is a state
of things that never lasts long, and the habit of over-
charging is easily acquired.

We heard some geese quack, and at once went in
search of the owner. She was discovered in a very
neat but small house, to which was attached a hen-
coop of gigantic proportions.

"Will you do me the honor to sell me some fat gos-
lings?" I inquired.

"Well," she answered, "I don't generally sell nothing till Christmas, but there ain't no law agin it, I guess."

"Good! If you will drive the flock up, I'll take my pick."

"Here, Matildy, drive them geese up here. Hurry up, now, and don't stop listenin' to their squawks!"

Matildy, a fine specimen of physical femininity, stopped for a moment to take a look at us, and then started for the shore, where the geese found plenty to eat. When the flock was penned, I picked out a goodly number, which were immediately caught, and most mercilessly deprived of their heads.

"Now, then, I want some chickens. Can I have them?"

"Would you as lief have hens?"

"No, madam, I have a great preference for youth. Old age is respectable, and should always be regarded with reverence, but in a hen it is not a popular attribute."

"Matildy, git some chickens."

And such a skittering was never seen. The screeching bipeds rushed hither and yon, while Matildy, who enjoyed the sport, lifted her garments to her knees with one hand, and, rushing into their midst, caught them with the other.

It was a very funny picture. The hens, aware of their fate, huddled together in one corner of the big coop, clucking to keep their spirits up, and hustling each other to get nearest the fence. Matildy, her black unkempt hair streaming down her shoulders, her coal-black eyes blazing with enjoyable excitement, crept stealthily up, her eye fixed upon the one she wanted, and then, at the right moment, made a most masterly dash, while the songsters flew and rushed at every possible angle with loud cries of fear, and managed every time to clutch the right one by head, or tail, or legs. She quietly passed it to the old lady, then drove the hens into another corner only to repeat the successful manœuvre.

At last I cried, " Hold, enough !" and by that time there was quite a pile of headless bipeds, who were to be promoted from common chickens to chicken-pie.

" Now then, how much for those geese ?"

" Well, I don't know. Do you think thirty cents apiece is too much ? If you do, why—"

" Oh, no ; don't take any thing off of that estimate. They wouldn't taste good if I got them any cheaper.

" And the chickens ; how much for them ?"

" Them chickens I didn't want to part with, and I'll have to charge you twenty-five cents a pair."

These are actual prices. Of course, we added to the silver a jackknife for the boy, and a few cigars for the gentleman who owned the estate, and then regarded the purchase as a ridiculously cheap one. I speak of this incident the more in detail, because it was the only landing-place on the coast where provisions were not as dear, or, in most instances, dearer than in New York or Boston. What the people at the various stations charge each other, I do not know ; but we found it impossible to get ice even, or any other provisions for the yacht, without being subjected to a process of extortion against which we more than once rebelled. Isaac's Harbor, however, is seldom visited by passing vessels. It is in the flower of Acadian innocence of those little games which wiser folks are accustomed to play. The people are slow, kind-hearted, and fearfully ignorant. There is no church in the village, and no school-house, and only those who are residents for a short time merely, and who come from other parts, take a newspaper.

The scenery is delightful. The wooded hills form a green background, and the little houses, scattered along the single street, present from the distance a very picturesque appearance. The chief source of income is a large "lobster factory," by what misnomer called so I could never understand, which is carried on by foreign talent. These simple people visit their pots twice a day, earning by hard work very small and uncertain wages, and yet seem to be perfectly content with their lot. When questioned as to their desire to be doing something better, to be engaged in business by which they can acquire a competency, they open their eyes in wonder, and stare at you as though you were talking in a dead language. No great ambition ever stirred them. They are quite content and happy with little, and would not take much trouble to get more.

These are fair samples of the inhabitants all along the coast. They are dull and sluggish, and can hardly be hired, even by the promise of glittering wages, to do any unusual work. They love their fishing-boats, and have become so accustomed to a diet of fish and lobsters that they can scarcely be persuaded to eat any thing else; and they have no purpose beyond setting a buoy or hauling a herring-seine.

"Now then, boys, for our first experience in camping out," I said that afternoon.

"Good enough," was the unanimous response.

"Halloo, there, forward!　Nimrod!"

"Aye, aye, sir!"

"Have you ever fished in this region?"

"Indeed I have.　There isn't a spot in this whole section of country as big as the palm of your hand where I haven't fished."

"Well, are there any trout here?"

"Trout? my goodness!　Why I've seen trout so thick here that you couldn't cross the stream for them bumping against your legs."

"Good! that's the place for us.　Get your traps ready; fold up your tent like an Arab"—he can enlarge the tents into a deformity better than any Arab I ever read about—"and we will all quietly steal away."

"Very good, sir."

"Say, Nimrod, any game in the woods?"

"Game?　I was out once rabbit-hunting, when I was actually chased back to my tent by 'em. I shot at 'em for two hours, till my powder was gone, and then I beat 'em on the head with a club."

"Ah!　Can we get just a couple for supper, do you think?"　Supper was a serious question with Nimrod, and he at once came down to solid facts, and said,

" I think Ah Bew "—that was his pronunciation—
" had better put us up a few things. I'll see to
it."

For half an hour we were tolerably busy. Knap-
sacks were filled with all the little necessities of careful
housekeeping, such as towels, tooth-brushes, and bed-
blankets, wolf-robes were tied up into the smallest
possible bundles, and we were ready.

Nimrod went ashore to engage the only two horses
in the village, carrying our truck with him, and we followed in the gig.

" Now, bundle your traps aboard the cart, gentlemen, for we have no time to lose ; we have eight miles
to travel over rough roads, and with horses whose very
best known speed is three and a half miles per—"

" Day," broke in Bertric.

With a lusty " get up !" and an impatient " get away !"
we started.

If the people were slow, the horses were quadrupe-
dal snails. A fair walk was the greatest speed we could
enforce by the most vigorous appliances.

" Boy," to the driver, " I'll give you a quarter if you
will make that brute trot for four consecutive minutes."

The boy looked in blank amazement, first at the
speaker, then at the shining quarter, and brought his
whip down on the ribs of the horse, making them resound like a drum. The beast seemed to be taken by
surprise, and actually made a motion as though he
would trot, but thought better of it, and settled back
into a more sullen walk than ever.

We resigned ourselves to the situation, and gave our

attention to the scenery, which was superb. The sun was sinking behind a bank of gray clouds, and when at last we reached the top of a knoll the country was spread out before us in undulating beauty, while in the far distance lay the harbor, with the *Nettie* lying quietly at anchor. Just then we entered the woods.

" I say, Nimrod, where are the rabbits?"

" Oh, they are further on."

" Yes, a good ways further," said Stigand.

" Are they, though? Look there! Stop your old horse, and let me out," said Fletch, in a whisper.

It was unnecessary to stop the horse, however, for Fletch half jumped and half slipped over the back-board, and was drawing a bead on something which only he could see.

" Bang!" sounded the smooth-bore, and then Fletch rushed into the bushes, from which he presently emerged bringing as a trophy a fine fat gray rabbit.

" There's our supper, at any rate."

" Didn't I tell you?" cried Nimrod.

" Jump aboard, Fletch ; it will be dark soon, and we want to get to a camping-ground as soon as possible."

We could hear the rushing streams in the near distance, and soon came upon one of the most romantic spots I ever beheld.

A hill, well wooded, and with huge timber trees, sloped gently down to the water. There was hardly any underbrush to obstruct either view or travel. Moss-covered monsters of the forests, the dead giants of olden times, stretched their sad lengths along the ground, while the woodpecker made the air resound with the noise of his search for food. The river, or stream, for it was hardly more than that, boiled and rushed along a sinuous path, singing its way to the sea. Here and there it broke into a fall that splashed upon the rocks below; and anon it hurried down the steep incline, like a crowd of merry fairies, tumbling over one another, and laughing all the while. Then again it settled itself into the quiet of a pond for a few rods, filling the deep gullies, in which the speckled treasures lay watching for the moths and bugs, which were struggling to get free.

"Now then, gentlemen, this is the spot in which to encamp. You, Stigand, take the axe, and cut us a straight pole, say about fifteen feet long, for the tent; and you, Bertric, take the hatchet, and cut some pins to fasten the ropes with."

"Well done, boys! Now give us a lift, and up she goes."

In a moment the tent was lifted in air, the side-ropes were pinned to the sod, and we had a cosy little house erected about ten feet in diameter.

For supper we had hard-tack, strong coffee, without milk or sugar, a roasted rabbit, and cheerful conversation. That was living fit for a king, and a great deal better than most kings enjoy.

We cut knots of pine which served us well for light. Sticking them in the ground, half a dozen of them in a semicircle in front of the tent, we passed the evening in enjoying the novelty of our situation, and at ten o'clock wrapped the drapery of our couches about us, and lay down to pleasant dreams.

Sunrise found us all awake.

"Nimrod, get my trout-rod and fly-book, and I will furnish you with a royal breakfast. By the way, Bertric, what's the matter with your face?"

"Matter enough," said Bertric. "I am all on fire. A good million of mosquitoes have been feeding on me all night, and my face feels like a section of the Alleghany Mountains."

Poor fellow! he was sadly bitten, and a sight to awaken pity in the most hardened heart. Numerous protuberances, great boulders of flesh, rose in uncomely grandeur all over his face. He had scorned the netting which the more careful had provided, and paid dearly for the neglect. I fumbled about my knapsack, found a bottle of ammonia, and soon managed to afford him some relief.

The great drawback of these woods is the armies upon armies of predatory insects. In the daytime you are encompassed by a cloud of black flies and their tiny relations, which the Indians call "no see 'ems," they are so small. But the bite—oh, the bite is the biggest part of them. At night these pests retire from the field, only to be replaced by enormous mosquitoes, which after a little render life entirely undesirable.

Up in Labrador they have a legend which, while it satisfactorily accounts for the existence of these creatures, does not for that reason reconcile you to their predations. It is said that a certain saint, I believe it was a woman, was banished from heaven for disobedience to the commands of one of the higher angels, and condemned to live in a lonely and uninhabited part of the earth. The angel who was ap-

pointed to carry out the sentence looked over the entire planet, but came across no spot so barren and
lonely as Labrador, to which place he conducted the
recreant. Time hung very heavy on her hands, as
one would naturally suppose. The contrast between
the Celestial City, with its genial companionship, and
the rugged shores of Labrador, was sufficiently great
to excite a sense of weariness. She prayed at length
that something might be sent her, even if it were only
a few flies. Her prayer was answered, and the mos-
quito, the buelôt, and the black fly were created.
That saint got more than she wanted, I suspect, and
I can not repress the feeling that the " higher angel "
was a little hard on her. At any rate, since that time
both saints and sinners alike have been bitten, until
human nature has invented certain strong explosives
with which to express its estimation of the gift.

" I say, Nimrod, what fly shall I use ? The brown
hackle or a white moth, or what ?"

" You had better try a black moth this morning."
He fumbled over my fly-book, and, picking out a delicate little fellow, made by Pritchard, said, " There, that
will kill finely, I suspect ; try him."

That delicate rod, which is the very apple of my
eye, and which I have used on so many expeditions
from the Adirondacks to the heart of Maine, was taken
out of its case with great care, and put together with
loving hands. It is a four-jointed rod, and weighs
only eleven ounces. It was made for me years ago
by a master workman, and one who had no little skill
as an angler. It was twelve feet and a half long, and
so well balanced that with care I could bring the tip

and the butt together. The butt was of straight-grained ash, and as fine a piece of wood as I ever saw. The second joint was of hickory, and the third of greenheart, while the tip was of elastic cane. It had whipped a great many streams, and killed more fish than I can count.

I fitted my click reel, on which was wound about forty yards of silk-and-hair line, into its accustomed groove, ran the line through the rings, and chose a delicate leader of gut about six feet long, to which I attached my black moth, and then felt ready for the prey.

Now, kind reader, go down with me to the stream. How it boils just here! It dashes over and by those rocks like a thing of life, but there's no use in casting the line just yet, for there are no trout here. Just below, down where those bushes hang over the stream and make a shade, there is a pool; it must be five or six feet deep, and eight or ten feet across, and in that pool is our breakfast, if I do not mistake. Now then, make no noise, for the true angler delights to come on his prey unawares. Can you see him? He is certainly there, waiting for us. He heads up stream, and is on the lookout for a little black moth that has accidentally wet his wings and finds it hard to fly. I will reel in my line, except about four or five yards, and try him. There, that moth dropped just right, and is floating down over his nose.

Heigh-ho! What a rush! He jumped clean out of the water. What a beauty he is! Did you see his silver belly and his crimson spots, as he flung the foam? I've got him well hooked. Now watch, for he'll fight hard before he comes to net. There, he makes a rush for the dead log yonder. If he gets under it, good-bye, trout. I will bend the rod backward, and give him the butt, for he is crossing the stream, where he will suck the bottom and stay in the sulks. He took out five or six yards of line, which must be reeled back, and then for another fight. Now I give him a slight pressure, pricking his mouth with the hook, and he's up and off again. He pulls hard, and as the space is very narrow, I give him the butt again, and keep a heavy strain on him. Now, then, he's tired out. Take the net, Fletch, and put it under him, as tenderly as though you were his mother. Good! now draw him out. How he kicks! but he's safe. There's our breakfast, boy, all secure.

He was safely landed, and when hung to the scales was found to weigh just two pounds and one ounce. No mean fellow for such a stream as this.

After the sun got up pretty high I found the brown hackle the most killing fly. We fished for a couple of hours, sometimes crawling through the bushes, and once in a while losing our temper as the line got caught in a branch just out of reach, and sometimes wading up to our waists in the middle of the current. Ah! but it was glorious sport. I did not think of the mosquitoes, but found it necessary on my arrival at the camp to use ammonia pretty freely. There was hardly a spot on my face as big as my finger-tip which was not ridged. Fletch was in the gayest of spirits, for it was his first experience in fly-fishing, and he had captured more than a dozen beauties. There are few things on earth that will compare in solid happiness with a thirty-minute fight with a two-pound trout, in a stream where there are coverts, and which ends in a successful capture.

We strolled through the woods in search of Nimrod's army of rabbits, but found none. The old man was rather crusty as we teased him about his enormous stories, but regained his good temper when we assured him that the trout paid us well for the trip.

Early in the afternoon we stowed our tent and bundles into the two wagons, and were deliberately dragged back to the village by the two Acadian horses. Hailing the *Nettie*, we were soon on board, tired but happy, and indulging in the luxury of fried trout and baked potatoes. Altogether it was a charming time, and we agreed to make a white mark against it in our memories and hearts.

CHAPTER VI.

LARKS AND A CHAT.

"Perhaps it may turn out a sang,
Perhaps turn out a sermon."
BURNS.

"For every inch that is not fool is rogue."
DRYDEN.

ETWEEN Country Harbor and the Gut of Canso we had no wind at all, and were literally given over to all sorts of pranks and practical jokes. There was never a day in the whole trip when we succeeded in subtracting so many years from our general average of forty-two, and in putting on the reckless habits of boyhood. Nothing seemed to be too daring, and nothing too foolish to do. At one time the whole company were climbing the shrouds, hand over hand, and hanging from various heights. There was a deep-seated rivalry among us to reach the topmast. Many were the struggles, the plunges, the kicks, as though somewhere in the air an invisible platform was placed, from which to get a fresh impulse, but to no purpose. We all got out of breath at nearly the same moment, and came sliding down to the deck with a rapidity which burned the cuticle from more than one hand. After a man

has expended the last ounce of energy in the upward
climb, it is curious how anxious he is to get back to
terra firma. He lets the rope slip through his fingers
in the most reckless way, and pays for his carelessness
with two or three blisters.

At another time we laid traps for each other, and
once in a while a man would get caught in a most
laughable and ridiculous predicament. Poor Stigand
was quietly walking across the deck, when unwittingly
he put his feet into a noose which lay in ambush, and
in an instant Bertric and Ruloff, who had rove the line
through a block at the foretop, hauled vigorously at
the other end. Stigand was fairly trapped. The rope
closed about his legs before he could extricate himself,
and in a moment more he was lying flat on his back,
while his pedals seemed about to take a trip to the
mast-head. Such a shout of derision followed the success of the trick that the victim struggled until he was
red in the face to get free. There are some events in
life, however, to which resistance only adds misery.
And this was one. Of course, the more he struggled
the taughter the line was held, and the higher his legs
ascended. When he had assumed a position almost
perpendicular, but with the wrong end up, Bertric
approached him to the music of the old song, " Come
into my parlor, said the spider to the fly."

" Well, here I am, Sir Spider. What is your gracious
pleasure," moaned Stigand.

" Do you forgive me for every thing I have ever
done to you ?" said Bertric.

" Yes, I'll forgive you, if you let me down before I
have a fit of apoplexy," said Stigand.

" And for every thing I shall do to you in the future ?" queried Bertric.

" Yes, yes, every thing," said Stigand.

" And do you forgive me for that ?" said Bertric
again, giving his victim a poke in the ribs.

" No, sir !" cried Stigand, struggling to get free. But
the rope had been fastened to the shrouds, and he was
evidently in for the whole play.

" Once more I ask, will you forgive me for that ?"
said Bertric, as he repeated the stroke.

" Yes, I forgive any thing and every thing," yelled
Stigand, growing purple.

" Then let him down," and Ruloff unfastened the
line.

Stigand got on his feet good-naturedly, and simply
said, " Bertric, I owe you one ;" and then quoted with
great effect a part of the little speech of Shylock :
" The villainy you teach me I will execute ; and it
shall go hard but I will better the instruction."

It was scarcely an hour before Stigand had ample
revenge. We had on board an overgrown fish-horn,
used to warn neighboring vessels in a fog. It was
fully six feet long, and from its awful mouth pro-
ceeded sounds terrible enough to scare the good temper from the sunniest constitution. When we were
all disposed to be quiet, and each, book in hand, had
taken his place in some shady part of the deck, under
lee of foresail or mainsail, Bertric, by some unlucky
chance, came across this instrument of musical torture,
and instantly saw larks in the distance.

He crept up behind me, as I lay absorbed in the
mysteries of Blunt's " Coast Pilot," and, placing the

mouth of the horn within six inches of my tympanum, blew a blast sufficiently sonorous to awaken the dead.

Heaven defend you, if you ever have such an experience. When reading a quiet and somewhat somniferous volume, like the one I have named, the mind naturally takes upon itself a calm and serene mood, and unsuspiciously views all things through the medium of its own repose. To be roused from such a condition by a blast that would do honor to the lungs of some indignant ogre is like waking up from a sound sleep with the cry of "Fire!" in your ears. I jumped to my feet in an instant, and turned upon the invader of my peace with as strong an expletive on my lips as I could lay hold of, and met his smiling countenance beaming on me with such an innocent sense of pleasure that the word died before it escaped the dental barrier; and simply murmuring those household words, "Let us have peace," lay down again to explore the labyrinths of Blunt.

Urged by his victory over me, he looked about for another victim on whom to expend his nervous energy. His eye fell on Stigand. Now this gentleman, scarcely recovered from the exhaustion incident to his performances on the tight rope, had satisfactorily disposed himself on the wolf-skin which he had placed on deck close to the skylight. Bertric took in the situation with all its possibilities at a glance. He managed to get down into the saloon unobserved, and, putting his horn through the skylight, and close to the recumbent Stigand, blew till his cheeks were in danger of bursting, then suddenly withdrew the horn. Stigand, who was writhing under the infliction, saw an opportunity for revenge. He got up quickly, and rushed to the cook's galley—

"Steward! a quart pot—quick!"

"Yes sir, yes sir," said Ah Boo, as he hurried to the hanging tins, and, selecting a tin quart pail, gave it to Stigand.

Stigand drew a bucket of salt water, filled the tin pail, and then quietly took his position at the skylight, as though nothing had happened. He heard the low chuckle of Bertric in the depths below, and waited patiently until his turn should come. Nor did he have to wait long, for Bertric, thinking that a good thing is worth doing twice, slyly pushed the horn through the skylight, and put it to his mouth for another blow.

By this time we all saw what was going on, and watched the issue with vast merriment.

No sooner had Bertric got the horn in position and opened his mouth for an effort, which, if it had been given, would have burst any tympanum of ordinary thickness, than Stigand emptied the entire contents of the pail into the hollow tube. The sound was just coming out, but it was met half-way by the all-conquering water. We heard a gulp, a sputter, a groan, as the liquid struck the lips, entered the mouth, and forced itself half-way down the throat of Bertric, who, taking the horn from his lips, was drenched from head to foot, and then we all broke out in a shout that made the welkin ring.

Bertric, however, does not easily lose his balance. He good-naturedly put his head out of the companion-way, and said, "Gentlemen, shall I get your umbrellas?

E 2

I think it is raining," and then retired to put on a dry suit of clothes.

" I think we are all boys to-day," I said to Ruloff, when the confusion had subsided.

" Well, and why not be ?" he answered. " We are men eleven months in the year, and can afford for a few weeks to go back to fifteen. A little fun hurts no man. Besides, you know the saying of that famous Greek ?"

" What was it ?" I inquired.

" That a man who isn't a fool half the time is a fool all the time," said Ruloff, with great emphasis. " We are enjoying the one half now, and I don't doubt it will enable us to be wise men the rest of the year. I have a theory that every man must at short intervals go back to fifteen, or he will never be able to bear fifty gracefully. Our boyhood ought to send its rays of laughter through our manhood, just as the Northern Lights shoot into the darkness of midnight. Tom Moore says that—

> ‘ Old Socrates, that pink of sages,
> Kept a pet demon, on board wages,
> To go about with him incog,
> And sometimes give his wits a jog ;’

and for the same purpose we keep the demon of fun, not ‘ on board wages,' but on board ship. To be grave at such a time as this is like turning Mother Goose into stately Latin."

" By the way," I said, " that last remark reminds me that it seems to have been a pleasant pastime for some of the quaint scholars of England to do exactly that thing."

" What thing ?" asked Ruloff.

" Why, translating Mother Goose into the vernacular of Jove and Venus. Nearly all of the old lady's verses have been funnily rendered, as, for instance, the famous story which begins with the ejaculation ' Hey, diddle, diddle,' and goes on with a pathetic recital of the prowess of the cow and the knavery of the dish."

" Indeed, and how does it sound in the tongue of Cicero ?" said Ruloff.

" Thus," I answered. " Listen to this piece of history when properly set up in Roman characters :

'Hei didulum, atque iterum didulum ! Felisque fidesque ;
Vacca super lunæ cornua prosiluit ;
Nescio qua catulus risit dulcedine ludi,
Abstulit et turpe laux cochleare fuga.'

" That," I continued, " was the work of no less a personage than Henry Douey, vicar of Wilton."

That same afternoon we were all sitting on the quarter-deck, thoroughly enjoying the scene as we hurried through the water, the spray being thrown on deck as far aft as the mainmast. The cold, gray shore, which not even the brilliant sunlight could charm into a bright mood, lay only three or four miles off. The dog seemed to have caught the spirit of the view, and lay at our feet dreaming of happy hunting-grounds.

" What are you thinking of, Bertric ?" said Algar, as he threw a coil of rope over the prostrate form of the former.

" Thinking of ? Do you imagine I can make the effort to think ? I am enjoying the very luxury of living ; I am thinking of nothing, and am happy."

" Good," broke in Ruloff; " I am in your condition.

I am in perfect repose, such as I always supposed Brahma enjoys as he sleeps the eternities away on a downy bed of clouds."

" Well," said Algar, " I have been guilty of wondering. I don't believe my brain is vigorous enough to actually think; but it has occurred to me to wonder what kind of vessels those sixteenth-century fellows made their trips in. How do you suppose they would compare with the *Nettie*, for instance? Does any body know?"

" For one," answered Stigand, " I am only interested in the Englishmen, who came across on the northerly line. The Spaniards went south, and my antislavery principles will not allow me to have any respect for them."

" Yes, yes; you are right," cried Bertric, managing to get up on his elbow—" you are right, Stigand. Take, for instance, that old salt—what's his name? Oh, yes, Gilbert; Humphrey was his cognomen, with a Sir prefixed—a very jolly old tar, who went down to the bottom after the most approved fashion. Can't some of you brush up your memories, and tell us about it? I had to learn it once for playing truant at school, and it gave me a taste for the sea which I haven't got over yet."

" I would like to have seen that sturdy old sailor, and have often wondered what he looked like," said Ruloff. " He must have been a bronze giant to endure all he went through."

" True," said Algar. " There is a pen-picture of him somewhere in English history. If I remember rightly, he was a person of prepossessing manners, and of such

noble bearing that you would have picked him out in
a crowd as a remarkable man. He was over six feet
in height, with an immense chest, and a voice that be-
tokened hearty good-nature. In complexion he was
rather light, and in temperament sanguine. He was
noted for his enthusiasm, his courage, his patriotism,
and, oddly enough, for his eloquence. Elizabeth was
so pleased with the success of his first voyage that she
gave him, as a mark of her royal esteem, an emblemat-
ical jewel. I think it was a small anchor of beaten
gold, with a large pearl at the peak; and he was so
proud of this mark of distinction that he ever after
wore it at his breast."

"Let me see," said Ruloff; "didn't Raleigh, who
did a handsome and very gentlemanly thing for Elizabeth, have something to do with that expedition?"

"No, I think not," said Algar, who was rubbing his
forehead to electrify some facts which seemed to have
a paralysis. "No, he came near going, but my impression is he backed out. Gilbert, who was a sort of half-
brother, started off alone."

"It was some time in June or July, and the year was
1583, when he turned his bows toward these shores,"
broke in Stigand. "At any rate, he landed in what is
now St. Johns in August of that year."

"And he had four or five vessels," said Ruloff, "not
one of which was nearly as large as the *Nettie*. I
wonder they were willing to trust themselves in the
middle of the Atlantic in such tubs."

"There, my friend, you are mistaken; for his biggest
vessel was the *Delight*, and she measured one hundred
and twenty tons, or just ten tons more than the one

we are in," cried Bertric, coming to the defense of Gilbert.

"Still," said Ruloff, "I insist that she was no larger than the *Nettie*, after all; for she was as blunt as a sperm-whale's head, and as flat in the bows as a three-story wooden house, and that counts for at least ten tons carpenter's measurement."

"But who knows the size of the other vessels?" I asked. "Does any one?"

"Does any one?" said Algar, defiantly. "You must remember the company you are in, sir. I can tell you the name and the tonnage of every vessel in that fleet."

"You can't do it," said we all at once.

"Now listen. There was the *Delight;* she was one hundred and twenty, and had a covered deck, and ran up to a point at the poop like a Chinese junk. Then there was the *Golden Hind*, which was only fifty tons. Then came the *Swallow*, of the same size. And, lastly, the *Squirrel*, which no respectable man would care to go round Cape Cod in, and she was only ten tons."

"Yes," said Ruloff, who had been cudgeling his brain, and raking up the almost forgotten lore of other days, redolent of birch and foot-ball and fireworks, "and on board those few vessels were two hundred and sixty men, who didn't care a rush-light for the New World, but only for the gold they thought to dig up. There were broken-down musicians, who wern't fit to grind a hand-organ, but who could twang the strings well enough to soothe the savage breast, and charm the gold ornaments out of his ears. For freight, Gilbert took toys with which to tickle the fancy of the noble red man, and, last, a lot of hobby-horses, for what earthly purpose I could never conceive."

"Good!" said Stigand; "just imagine a wild Indian on the coast of Nova Scotia, brandishing a scalp in one hand, while with the other he held the reins and guided the uncertain steps of a hobby-horse. What an imposing picture! It only needs the war-whoop to make it complete."

"Gentlemen, we'll have no levity, if you please," I said, with stern severity. "I am anxious to know the fate of those craft."

"Well, the company no sooner landed than they got into a row. There was no gold to be had; and though they passed a fleet of more than one hundred vessels engaged in the sedentary occupation of the cod-fishery, they concluded not to get a living in an honest way, but fell to cutting each other's throats—an occupation which does not conduce to a successful enterprise."

"But the vessels?" asked Bertric.

"The *Delight*, their stand-by, was lost soon after their arrival, and the *Swallow* was sent home with a score of sick men on board. A while after, the party started for Europe in the *Golden Hind* and the *Squirrel*. The *Squirrel* was the flag-ship, with Gilbert on board."

"I can't conceive why such a shrewd old fellow as he should choose a boat of ten tons for a flag-ship in which to cross the ocean," said Stigand.

"Exactly," answered Bertric; "but perhaps the *Golden Hind* was a little soft in her timbers, or, better still, perhaps the old gentleman wanted to spend the time with the smallest number; for it must be confessed that his expedition was made up of the raggedest and most villainous set of men that could be scraped out of the slums of a British seaport."

"Yes, but Gilbert died splendidly; and that last scene off the Azores used to make my blood tingle," said Ruloff.

"If the story is true," broke in Algar, "it was certainly heroic. He was sitting on deck in a storm, and when the little tea-cup of a craft was swallowed, he was heard to say, 'Cheer up, boys; we are as near to heaven by sea as by land.'"

"That strikes me as being very heroic," said Bertric; "and it touches the highest note of that daring which has shed lustre upon those two centuries of adventure. But why do you say, 'if true?'"

"Why?" replied Algar; "because there is an air of improbability about the whole story, and an actual impossibility connected with that part of it."

"No, no, no, no," we all chimed in; "you can't break our image down in that way. You heretical iconoclast! the story is too good not to be true. The internal evidence is in its favor."

"The internal evidence is against it, as you shall confess," said Algar, defiantly. "Now listen. 'He was heard to say, "Cheer up, boys,"' etc. Is not that the way the story runs? and doesn't History herself laugh when she puts those words in his mouth?"

"Certainly he was heard to say it," we answered.

"And by whom was he heard?" queried Algar.

"Why, by those on board the *Golden Hind*, to be sure," said we.

"Ah, indeed!" said Algar; "how far off do you suppose the *Golden Hind* was at that moment? Not less than one hundred yards, at least; and even that proximity would have been exceedingly dangerous."

"Well, what then?" we said.

"Only this," he replied, "that in an Atlantic gale, when the wind was blowing hard enough to blow the *Squirrel* to Davy Jones's locker, the remark which Sir Humphrey is said to have made could not have been heard. Why, when the wind is blowing hard, and the *Nettie* is swashing into the sea, you can hardly hear the captain give his orders—and that when a man has been stationed amidships to catch them and hurl them forward. And how is a vessel that is a full hundred yards off going to hear a passing remark which is made by a captain to his own men? You see the thing is false on the face of it."

"Yes—but history," began Stigand.

"Oh, pshaw! what is history?" said Algar. "I don't believe every thing I hear—do you?"

"Supper ready, sir," said Ah Boo; and so ended the tilt. Who had the better of the contest I leave you to decide.

CHAPTER VII.

A SAND-BANK AND A FIGHT.

"And, departing, leave behind us
Footprints on the sands of time."
LONGFELLOW.

"In peace there's nothing so becomes a man
As modest stillness and humility;
But when the blast of war blows in our ears,
Then imitate the action of the tiger:
Stiffen the sinews, summon up the blood."
SHAKESPEARE.

 HE wind was light all the next day, and it seemed as though we should never get beyond the ragged rocks of Nova Scotia; but in the early afternoon we sighted White Head, and by four o'clock, with a gentle breeze, managed to run it down.

While we were sailing on so smoothly I said to the captain,

"Cap, where away does Sable Island bear from here?"

"Let me see," he replied, pondering, and taking his direction from the compass; "about there, I should say," pointing with his hand; "as nigh E.S.E. as you can make it out. And a horrible place it is."

Sable Island is a great curiosity, whose history is lit-

tle known by the people at large. It is a bank of sand,
situated about one hundred miles from the mainland,
and right in the track of vessels from Europe. It is
about thirty miles long, and one and a half in width,
and presents the general shape of a bow. By what
force or forces it ever came to thrust its head up above
water, and insist upon being called land, when by good
rights it ought to be a part of the bottom of the sea,
no one can tell. On the north of the island there are
as many as sixty fathoms of water, and not many miles
to the southward it deepens to three hundred fathoms.
This vast sand-hill rises from this enormous depth just
for the sake of getting in the way of navigation. It
subserves no other conceivable purpose than to be-
guile unwary craft into its shoal waters, and keep them
there until they go to pieces. It is so cunning in its
geological demonism that, instead of lifting its front
like a cliff from the sea, that the inward and outward
bound might be warned of its proximity, it lies very
low, only a few feet above the surface, assuming a dull
gray color, not unlike the ocean in a cloudy day, and
stretches its shoals out for miles, with only six or ten
feet of water on them ; so that when a vessel thinks she
has given the island a good berth, just then her keel
grinds on the sand, and the ship and cargo are lost to
a certainty, while the passengers must struggle with a
heavy and remorseless surge in order to save their
lives. It always seemed to me, as I looked at it on
the chart, like Victor Hugo's devil-fish lying on
the water, with his smooth but treacherous back just
above the surface, and his little hillocks of eyes peering around the horizon for a stray sail, while his long

tentacles of shoals are stretched out for sixteen miles in one direction and twenty-eight in another, a dangerous foe to all passers-by.

And great spoil the sandy monster has had in times past. Of late years such a wholesome dread of it has pervaded the minds of our merchants that they have changed the course of their vessels, which now sail along a more southerly line, and so keep out of its reach. But the stories it could tell of shipwreck and disaster would make the world's blood curdle in its veins, while each particular hair would stand on end in horror. It is worth your while, if you are not well up in geography, to take down the atlas, and look out this weird monster of the deep. You will find it due south from Cape Breton.

The surface of the island, which is composed of sand without a rock, is low and undulating, like a Western prairie. Throughout its length and breadth there is not a single tree or good-sized shoot to be found. Its only productions are a strong kind of grass, known as seamatweed, with here and there a whortleberry patch and some cranberry bushes. Even the grass refuses to grow, except in the low places by the shore, where it is continually washed by the incoming waves. When the wind blows a gale, the loose sand is borne aloft like a cloud, sometimes even burying, as a waterspout does when it strikes an unfortunate vessel, those poor shipwrecked creatures who are looking about for a shelter. When the wind dies away, you find here and there conical hills from fifty to a hundred feet high, which have been piled up by the capricious northwester, and which during the next week, perhaps, will be taken up again almost bodily by the gale and deposited in another part of the island. It is a huge graveyard with shifting sepulchres, for even the dead are allowed no rest. Their bones are exposed by every storm, and hurried here and there to be reburied again by the changing sands when the gale is over.

It is said that no one who has not actually witnessed a storm on this frightful spot can even imagine its horrors. The mountainous waves come rolling over the great deep with the steady tread of an army corps of giants in a battle-charge, their white crests floating in the wind, and strike this thirty miles of shore with such a shock that the whole island sensibly vibrates beneath one's feet, while the thunder of the dashing waters sends dismay to the stoutest hearts. The whole southern end is covered with timber, which has either been driven thither by the current or torn from wrecks and hurled ashore.

The Marquis de la Roche was the first man who visited this island with an intention to colonize. By the orders of Henry IV., he sailed from France in 1598, carrying with him a number of convicts. It was a notable custom in the Old World to ship off its unruly elements, and to sow them in the fields of the New World like dragon's teeth. The Marquis intended at first to land his precious freight of rogues on the Nova Scotia coast, and to start a nice little piratical village, with himself as the head of the Ring. By some unfortunate chance, however, he sighted Sable Island on his way, and it struck him that, being a somewhat secluded spot, he would make his first experiment there. He consequently landed his forty thieves, and then started to make explorations along the coast to the westward, intending to give his little colony a call on his way back. He was driven by stress of weather, and compelled to return to France without the expected visit.

The convicts had a rough time of it, and learned by heart that passage of the Scriptures which says that the way of the trangressor is hard. They had plenty of time for meditation, but nothing to eat, and no roof for their heads. They would have miserably perished had not a French ship run on the sand-bar, and stuck fast until she went to pieces. They found on board provisions to supply their wants for a time, and some sheep, which they killed, as they were pressed by hunger. From the torn timbers of the wreck they formed huts, which they thatched with the briers and grass of the island.

Seven years after, when Chetodol, the pilot of De la Roche, was sent by the king to bring them back to France, only twelve were found alive. They were dressed in the skins of the seals they had managed to kill, and were altogether in such a squalid and distressing condition that the royal heart was moved by their story of privation to give them a gratuity of fifty crowns each. The pilot, with an eye to business, had kept very still about the king's orders, and, as though he had only chanced on shore, promised to take them aboard his vessel if they would give him all the skins they had collected, which they willingly agreed to do. They, however, discovered the fraud, and after their return to France instituted against him a lawsuit, which ended in the recovery of large damages, with which they were enabled to enter into trade with the Indians.

Some time afterward the Portuguese, out of their pity for the distresses of those who had the misfortune to strike keel on these inhospitable sands, landed a lot of calves, which in a few years stocked the island; but, such is man's unprincipled love of gain, a horde of adventurers killed them all off for the sake of their hides and tallow; or, rather, for three generations gangs of men visited the place, summer after summer, and hunted until the last beef was killed. A second time the island was stocked, and a second time the cattle were all destroyed. This excited such indignation in the hearts of all generous people that a proclamation was issued by Governor Armstrong at Annapolis, forbidding these predations under penalty of a severe sentence, which caused a lull in the robberies for a time. At length, however, the old habits were resumed, and the island was once more left to the mercy of marauders.

Subsequently were landed from a wreck a number of ponies, sturdy little fellows, who seemed to have an appetite for sand and sea-matweed. They multiplied vigorously for a great many years, and at last increased beyond the means of support. Then, again, some rabbits and some hogs drifted ashore, and with them a few score of rats — so the wrecked mariner could have a course dinner after the custom of his native land. If a Frenchman, he could dine off a Shetland pony, with tenderloin steak and a roast rib; if a Chinaman, and he wanted a good bill of fare, he could stew the rats to his heart's content, and while picking the juicy bones dream of the flowing pigtail of his father in Hong Kong; if an Englishman, he could shoot a young steer, and make plans for the future over his slice of roast beef.

Since the beginning of this century a superintendent with several employées have been stationed on the island, supplied with sufficient means to render assistance, and to provide comfortably for those who are driven ashore. A government vessel visits the place at stated intervals, to keep up the necessary stock of provisions, clothing, and medicines, and to take off the shipwrecked. Still it is not the place that would be chosen for a summer residence, but only a wild, weird, ghostly sand-bank, that will have many a story to tell on the morning of the resurrection.

"Now then," said the pilot, who had been listening attentively to our talk of Sable Island, and who had knowingly, nodded assent to our descriptions of the place, "as soon as we get clear of Roaring Bull Rock, we will turn the yacht's nose to the norrard, and get into still water. Halloo! there comes a whiff."

We had been lazily lounging along for such a length of time that it was an inexpressible relief to see the sail fill, and feel the *Nettie* heel over. Little Canso Light is situated on an exceedingly picturesque island, and stands out against the sky to the eastward, as one turns toward the north, with its alternating zones of black and white. The larger craft find it necessary to keep well off shore in passing it, because of the reefs and ledges whose ragged edges would have little mercy on a vessel; but our best course was inside and to the westward, and we soon found ourselves as by magic in a good lee, and keeping company with a score or two of lumbermen, fishing-vessels, and other craft. The entrance to the harbor of Little Canso is all we could wish, while the exit is through a channel so narrow that you can throw a biscuit to either shore. The village consists of possibly fifty houses, and their chief business seems to be the supply of vessels to and from the fishing-grounds of the Gulf. To eke out a living beyond that afforded by the barter indicated—such as the sale of hob-nailed boots that wear out in a fortnight, because they are provided in unstinted generosity with brown-paper soles, and the occasional disposal of woolen shirts, which with ordinary use will last until they are washed, and which at that critical moment emulate the example of the parson's "one hoss shay," and simply vanish into shreds—they cure innumerable cod-fish. That esculent is to be found in quantity in every spot on the coast where two or three houses assume the style of a village. It greets you at every anchorage, and on the whole has a tendency to effect a decline in your appetite for a breakfast of that generally toothsome material.

We gave the town a gun as we passed, by way of " How do you do," and then shot like an arrow through the narrow passage and out into the still and delightful waters of Chedebucto Bay. The dog grew restless the moment the land became a possibility to his canine consciousness; and when it came up within fair swimming distance, he put his paws on the rail, snuffed the air from the hills, and set up a piteous howl, which made us feel that in some former stage of his existence he had been a fisherman, or, better still, a shopkeeper,

F

who, as a penalty for his iniquity, had been doomed to pass ten or twelve years inside the ribs of a quadruped. At any rate, we were compelled to hold him by the collar to keep him from landing.

We sailed across Chedebucto Bay, seventeen miles, in just an hour and twenty minutes. Away off on the right, like a ghostly shore, rose the dim outlines of Cape Breton, while on the left was Eddy Point Light, at the entrance of the Big Gut of Canso. About fifteen miles from the entrance is Port Mulgrave, where we expected letters, and at half-past seven we came up to the wind and dropped anchor.

" Down with the boat, boys, and we'll soon hear from home."

These were cheering words, and in ten minutes we were climbing up the ladder on the wharf, and in less time than it takes to write it we were breaking open sundry envelopes, and getting the first news from those we had left behind.

This Gut of Canso is certainly one of the pleasantest spots on earth in summer. We had long ago wearied of the clay slates and other metamorphic rocks of Nova Scotia, grand in their barrenness, and were delighted with the refreshing and many-shaded green of the richer soil to the north. It was like coming suddenly from stony and unproductive fields into a ·fragrant flower-garden.

We were all the more interested in Port Mulgrave because it is diagonally opposite Port Hastings, which is on the Cape Breton side of the Gut, and the terminus of the Atlantic Cable, and the beginning of the lines of the Western Telegraph. An incredible number of operators live in a large square wooden house there, and their cunning fingers are kept constantly busy transmitting messages to the East and West.

We saw there one of the most remarkable dogs I have ever heard of. He must not be forgotten in this narrative. He was a pure Newfoundlander, of the short-haired species. The long-haired dogs are not looked upon with much favor by those who have an eye more to the practical value than to the beauty of the animal. Nothing certainly is more dignified or majestic of mien, save perhaps the St. Bernard, than the shaggy, full-grown, and well-bred Newfoundland dog ; but he is almost valueless as a retriever, since his long hair holds so much water that he is soon tired out, and easily catches cold.

We were all standing on the wharf when the owner of the canine came up, and said very courteously,

" Did you ever see a dog dive and swim under water, sir ?"

" Certainly not," I replied.

With that introduction to a very curious exhibition, he whistled Dick to his side. The wharf was about six feet out of water, and the water was about seven feet deep. The owner seemed to be on very intimate terms with the animal, saying to him,

" Now, Dick, I want you to do your level best. Do you hear, sir ?"

Dick wagged his tail, as though he perfectly comprehended the remark, and announced that he was ready for the ordeal by sundry low growls, which none but his master could interpret.

Taking a flat stone in his hand, the gentleman

showed it to the dog, saying, " Now, Dick, I want you to bring that up from the bottom;" and then gave it a toss.

Dick watched it with eager eyes as it fell with a splash, and sidled its way, now in one direction and now in another, to the bottom, then with a leap he struck the water just above where the stone fell, swam to the bottom, grasped it in his teeth, and brought it in triumph to the surface.

" That 'ere dorg is mor'n half fish," was the criticism of a bystander; and this so perfectly expressed our own convictions that we silently patted Dick on the head, and gave him a cracker as a reward of merit.

" Now then, Nimrod," I said next morning, " where can we get some salmon-fishing ?"

" In the Margaree River," he promptly replied. " I have just come from there, and had very good luck. I caught several fish weighing over twenty pounds, and I think you will not be sorry if you go there."

" Margaree River ? John, get out the chart, and we will study geography."

" I say, pilot, is there enough water to float us at the mouth of the Margaree ?"

" No, sir, there's just water enough to run you on a bar. It's an awful harbor, with no lee."

" Yes—but we want some salmon."

" Well, you can go to Port Hood, that's mor'n forty mile to the suth'ard, where we can anchor, and you can take teams, and go on overland."

That struck us as a good idea, and we thought it would be larks to take a trip of that kind. It would vary our experience in a charming way.

Very late that night we arrived at Port Hood, which is not a good place to enter in the dark. You take your course mainly by soundings, finding the channel, and keeping in it, if you can, which with the wind ahead is not an easy thing to accomplish. I advise you, if you ever go there, to go in the daytime. We ran along for some time in water of eleven feet—we drew eight and a half—with the feeling that any unevenness in the surface of the bottom would bring us up all standing. Once we just scraped. We could feel the grinding of the keel, but the yacht had headway enough to carry us over the bar into deeper water. We came to anchor at ten o'clock under Smith Island.

The next day was absolutely perfect. The sun was warm and unclouded, and the water of the harbor was as smooth as glass. Several school of mackerel were flipping, one not ten rods off. We quickly got bait ready, with which to tole them alongside, and in a few minutes hundreds and even thousands were playing about the vessel. Our jigs were out, and such sport as we had in the next thirty minutes it is not easy to describe. The beauty of mackerel fishing is that you neither have to bait your hook nor take your fish off. Brighten your jig by scraping it with a knife, and you have done enough to attract the greedy eyes of this fine fish. Throw your bait over, and then your jig into the midst of it, and before you know it a fish has the hook in his mouth. Haul in with a rapid but a gentle and loving hand, for the fellow's jaws are very tender, and when on board give your line a sudden twitch, and the fish falls off and leaves you ready for the next trial. So the fun continues as long as the school remains; but this is mere matter of chance, for mackerel are shy fish withal, and any sudden shout, or noise of any kind, and you hear that peculiar swash which informs you that they have all taken the alarm and are off. We caught something like a hundred and twenty-five in the thirty minutes in which our visitors lingered near us, and at the end of the thirty-first minute the water, which had been alive with them, was as quiet as though there were not a mackerel within a thousand miles.

While Ruloff was ashore looking up a team to carry us to the Margaree, which we afterward learned was forty-four miles distant, I went down to my books to look up any information that was to be had on the subject of Cape Breton.

"An Impartial Frenchman," as he calls himself, published in 1760, about the time the American colonies were beginning to effervesce under the subtle influence of that yeast of progress called Liberty, a history of the island, which is a very good book of reference, but a terribly dry volume to read on a summer's day. He talks somewhat statistically about what he calls the "Gulph of St. Laurence," which phrase makes one feel that the river is the throat and the lakes the several stomachs of a watery giant, who takes pleasure in that enormous mouth with which at one gulp he disposes of the craft that confidingly trust to his protection. This writer may have been exceedingly impartial for a Frenchman, but his statements are not true when looked at from the Anglo-Saxon angle of vision. The island, he tells us, is " covered with lakes, rivulets, and bogs." To the contrary, we found it, after our long ride, one of the most picturesque of places. In the extreme north there are a few settlements only, and the original woods hold sway, divided by deep rivers, which are well stocked with salmon and various kinds of trout.

Cape Breton is a triangular piece of land, so situated that it becomes the natural key to the Gulf of St. Lawrence. St. Lawrence Bay is the apex in the north; Madame Island forms the southwest corner, and Scatari Island the southeast corner. Its greatest length is about one hundred miles from north to south, and its greatest breadth about eighty miles, which gives an area, exclusive of the surface of the lakes, of something like two million acres for the woodsman's axe and the plow and spade of the farmer.

The coast on the south and east is serrated, affording innumerable harbors to the captain who knows the way in, and an equal number of chances for shipwreck for the vessel that must find a lee whether or no. The shore is very bold in many places, huge cliffs of solid rock jutting far out into the sea, with reefs and solitary rocks, over which the water breaks continually. The island is said to be very rich in coal; and I learn it from good authority that, between Miray Bay and the entrance to the Bras d'or Inlets, there are one hundred and twenty square miles of land containing veins of coal that can be worked with profit. Fortunes have already been made in this enterprise, but there are many more fortunes of equal bulk waiting to be picked up by some rash and daring companies.

The island was discovered by Cabot, and was either

called Breton by him, in honor of Britain, or by Verraz-
zani, a subsequent explorer in the service of France,
after Brittany in his native land. Its first inhabitants
were probably Frenchmen, who used to come from
Newfoundland and Nova Scotia in the first decade of
the eighteenth century, and live in huts during the
summer months, when they pursued the trade of
codding; but in winter it was given over to the tender mercies of the fur-hunters and purchasers. It was
then a howling wilderness, with no white population
any where except on the coast. The interior was a
terra incognita so far as the white man was concerned,
but was sparsely inhabited by the Mic-Macs, who
seem to have spread themselves over Prince Edward's, Newfoundland, and Cape Breton in profuse
abundance.

The French, soon after their settlement, knowing
that both England and the colonies situate on Massachusetts Bay were looking at the island with longing
and envious eyes, began the fortification of Louisburg,
on the southeast coast. Not content with this, they
instigated the Indians to make sundry attacks on the
English settlers who had pre-empted the shore along
the Gut of Canso, then called the Gut of Fronfac, until
at last it became necessary to settle the question of
rightful possession by the stern arbitrament of the
sword. The government of Massachusetts determined
to rout the French from Louisburg at any cost, and
the war in which this deed of prowess was accomplished is of such importance that I shall be excused
if I give it something more than a passing notice.

Louisburg was in 1745, or thereabouts, the strongest

fortification on the continent, with the exception, possibly, of Quebec. It consisted of a rampart of stone, nearly forty feet high, and two miles and a half in circumference. It had also a ditch of nearly the same length, and eighty feet wide. Thirty million livres had been expended on the structure, but, like some of our city buildings, and perhaps for the same reason, it had never been completed.

When the attack was determined upon, the war took upon itself the semblance of a religious war. It was a crusade in favor of the cod-fishery and against the papacy. No wonder that New England was all aglow. It required only two months to enlist 3200 men from Massachusetts, 500 from Connecticut, and 300 from New Hampshire, besides 300 from Rhode Island, who were not in the fight. It was a volunteer army, made up of farmers and mechanics; but they were drilled by common interest and danger, which is sometimes better than Hardee's Tactics.

The flag that was used on the battle-field was presented to the itinerant preacher George Whitefield, who roused New England blood to the boiling point of religious enthusiasm by having inscribed upon it the motto, " Nil desperandum Christo duce." This reverend gentleman entered into the spirit of the crusade by sermon and prayer, and scattered his peace principles to the wind until Louisburg fell, when he gathered the pieces together again, and went on his way rejoicing.

It was necessary to have a leader for an expedition of this kind, and William Pepperell, of Kittery, Maine, was chosen. He was a merchant, extensively concerned in trade, and so popular that for thirty-two successive years he was elected one of His Majesty's council for the province of Massachusetts. He had little or no military education, except that which had been thrust upon him by constant conflicts with neighboring Indians.

On the 4th of April the troops embarked for Canso, where they arrived in safety, after having suffered from the fogs and storms of the Nova Scotia coast. On the 13th of April the fleet, augmented by the command of Commodore Warren, who had arrived from his station in the West Indies, sailed into Chaparouge Bay, and landed its men, who at once drove the surprised Frenchmen within their lines of fortification.

By the 7th of May the town was fairly invested, and a summons was sent to Duchambon to surrender. It was a pretty tough fight from that time until the 16th of June. The fortunes of the armies were various. Unheard-of exploits were accomplished by the New-Englanders, while the French exhibited both tact and courage. Five several charges were made on the fortifications, none of which were successful, though in the last one the colonists lost 189 men. After that, however, Commodore Warren engaged, and after a fearful struggle captured, the *Vigilant*, a seventy-four, and 560 soldiers, which spread such consternation among the Frenchmen that they were completely demoralized, and, just as the colonial troops were gathering their strength to make a decisive onslaught, Duchambon thought the matter over and concluded to surrender.

The flag of Whitefield had done its work, and was

planted victoriously on the ramparts. The civilians had shown themselves worthy to meet well-trained soldiers, and to wrest the day from their grasp. 4130 prisoners were taken, of which number 650 were veterans, and 1310 belonged to the militia. As Mr. Martin says in his little history of Nova Scotia and Cape Breton, " Not the least singular event connected with this gallant circumstance was the fact that the plan for the reduction of this regularly constructed fortress was drawn up by a lawyer, and executed by a body of colonial husbandmen and merchants."

The siege of Louisburg lasted forty-nine days, and it must be confessed that the result would have been very different but for several favoring circumstances. In the first place, the weather was not only unusually but remarkably fine. If it had rained, the little army of besiegers, who spent a great part of their time working like oxen to drag the heavy guns across the bogs intervening between the shore and the fortifications, would undoubtedly have suffered greatly. Not only would their work have been impeded and indefinitely delayed, but sickness would have inevitably thinned their ranks. In the second place, the troops inside the fortress were in very ill-humor, even to the verge of insubordination. If they had been a unit, they could have made successful sorties from their stronghold, and put to rout or thrown into confusion the besiegers. In the third place, by a very curious coincidence, nearly every British man-of-war stationed along the coast found its way into the harbor.

The following ships of the line and frigates arrived during the siege, and helped, of course, to completely demoralize the enemy: The *Superbc*, 60 guns; the *Lancaster*, 40; the *Mermaid*, 40; the prize *Vigilant*, 64; the *Princess Mary*, 60; the *Hector*, 40; the *Chester*, 50; the *Canterbury*, 60; the *Sunderland*, 60; the *Lark*, 40.

There were, then, more than five hundred guns bearing on the noble fortification, and it is little wonder that Duchambon's heart grew depressed to the point of surrender as he saw this formidable fleet come in one after another, and anchor within short range.

After the memorable capture, General Pepperell gave a dinner to which Commodore Warren and the officers of the navy were especially invited. It so happened that the Rev. Samuel Moody, chaplain of the General's regiment, was present, and must needs be asked to pray for a blessing. This gentleman had such a wonderful gift for long prayers, with which he was accustomed to wear out the patience of the most long-suffering, that the officers were in a quandary for fear the soups and meats would all be cold before he could be induced to say Amen. He was one of those clergymen who leave their amen at home, and so continue indefinitely. It would never do to speak to him on the subject, for he is reported as being as irritable and crusty as he was prolix. The diners-out, however, were surprised and delighted when the chaplain, who was at a loss for the first time in his life, rose in his place and delivered the following model prayer: "Good Lord, we have so many things to thank thee for that time will be infinitely too short to do it; we must, therefore, leave it for eternity. Bless our food and fellowship on this joyful occasion, for the sake of Christ our Lord. Amen."

Several important consequences followed this re-markable victory. It gave to England the key to the whole Gulf of St. Lawrence ; it broke up what was fast becoming a very important French naval station, for in the November preceding the capture a magnificent French fleet, consisting of three huge men-of-war, six East Indiamen, nine brigantines, thirty-one other ships, and two schooners, found there a safe anchorage, and sailed thence for purposes of trade or war ; and, beyond all this, it effectually destroyed the hold of France on the Western continent, thus, perhaps, altering the his-tory of all coming time.

General Pepperell and Commodore Warren were made Baronets of Great Britain, the troops went home, and another bloody page was inserted between the covers of that book which records the progress of mankind toward a general peace, which is apparently to be reached only after sprinkling the soil of the planet with the gore of patriots.

Cape Breton is so far north that its winters are te-diously long, while its summers are a mere flash in the pan. Whatever grows must take time by the forelock, or the first frost will nip it in the bud. Ambitious crops which expect to be garnered must get under full headway by the middle of June, and take advantage of every warm day in July and August, for with the first of September the nights begin to grow chilly, and after that the ground becomes stubborn, and refuses to give any more nourishment. Few flowers, except those of the hardier sort, shed their fragrance on the air, and fruits of nearly all kinds positively refuse to ripen.

There is still game in the woods, if one has sufficient

toughness of cuticle to defy the armies of insects. These are, however, so formidable that few venture far from the coast until snow falls, and their prowess is so great that their depredations are recited in heroic verse. We heard of some sailors who, being determined on fresh meat, made a journey of a few miles into the back country after caribou. They were so beset by an immense cloud of mosquitoes that they were forced to beat an orderly retreat. Not content with driving the invaders out of their dominions, the enemy, by a masterly flank movement, hemmed them in on deck, and presented their little bills with such effect that the sailors were fairly driven below, and compelled to batten down the hatches. The mosquitoes were plucky to the last, for they drove their bills through the hatches, and the sailors, with axes and hammers, clinched them on the inner side — so the story runs—thus proving over again the old truism that brains are superior to brute force.

Very few bears are to be seen, but caribou are plenty in the season. They are best captured when the snow is a couple of feet deep in the woods. The hunters then kill them by the score. With snow-shoes they can easily tire out the game, which sinks at every spring to its shoulder. Our "Impartial Frenchman" must have had some sport of this kind in the olden days, for he tells us that "the flesh of this beast is eatable; and, indeed, it makes as good soop as beef." He describes another animal, however, which no hunter likes to meet, and his imagination or his fear must have supplied him with facts, for the wild-cat, when full-grown and ferocious, is apt to make one's heart palpitate in the most distressing way. I have killed almost every thing in the way of game, and have no more of the ingredient of fear in my composition than the average hunter, but whenever I have seen a wild-cat, especially if he has arrived at maturity, and I have reason to think his claws full-grown, I have let him alone. He is a creature whose intimacy I studiously avoid. I confess I am afraid of him, and this fear springs from an experience I had once, when I was under twenty. I was out after bears, and had suc-ceeded in sending my leaden compliments in the shape of a ball weighing a good ounce into his fore-shoulder, bringing him down, and giving me a good right to his pelt, when I heard a rustle in a tree about fifty feet off. I looked up and saw those two yellow sparkles which make one feel that he is in the presence of the evil one himself. A huge wild-cat was cozily tucked up on one of the higher limbs watching the scene be-low, and had just made up his mind to have a tilt with me. At that moment I thanked God for breech-load-ers, and I feel reasonably certain that but for that fact the people would have been spared a great many poor sermons. Quicker than I can describe it I took two cartridges from my pouch, and thrusting one into the gun, held the other in my left hand for an emer-gency. If ever I took a careful as well as a rapid aim, it was at that moment. The beast was on his haunch-es ; he showed his teeth, and began to move his fore-feet nervously, pattering them down on the limb, as is the habit of the brute before he springs. A sharp re-port, and then, hardly looking at the result, I reloaded. It was very fortunate that I did so, for the cat had been hit in the abdomen only, and, just as I was ready for him, he made a jump for me, landing within five feet of the place where I stood. I have never said so before, but I am now ready to confess that every individual hair of my head stood on end, and I wished most heartily that I hadn't concluded to hunt that morning. Whether it was that my first bullet began to produce its effect, or whether the fall was greater than he expected, I know not, but the cat was perhaps ten or fifteen seconds gathering himself up and getting ready for another spring, which would have been equivalent to my funeral, and that saved me. I put the second ball into him, and he lay still.

Since that time I have had no ambition whatever to engage in a personal encounter with wild-cats. They shall never smell powder from my gun, if they will be kind enough to keep on their own side of the fence.

My impression is that our "Impartial Frenchman" must have had the same electrical effect produced on his capillaries, for he writes in the most confused way about the natural history of this quadruped. He says, "The quincajou resembles a large cat. His hair is of a red brown, and the tail so very long that, when he turns it up, it makes two or three curls on his back. This is his offensive weapon. With it he entwines the poor animal, after first seizing him with his paws; then he bites him in the neck under the ear, and does not let go his hold until the victim is dead." If that sentence was not written by a man who had at some time in his life been pretty badly scared, then I can make no diagnosis of the diseased condition that produced it.

Port Hood is one of the three or four good anchor-

ages of the west coast of Cape Breton. It is very
beautifully situated on a kind of bluff, and its few
hundred inhabitants live mostly on a single street or
road that runs parallel with and faces the water. Immediately in front of the village are the two islands,
Smith and Henry, which serve as a breakwater for the
harbor, which in ordinary blows is as smooth as a mill-
pond. The people are mostly fishermen—that is, they
depend largely for support on the products of the
water, though they nearly all have little farms which
they work at odd times. The women are often seen
in the fields handling the rake and the hoe as though
they were accustomed to those implements, and so the
grounds are kept in good order while the liege lords
hold an intermittent correspondence with Neptune by
occasionally " dropping a line." They are a snugly
housed, and, on the whole, thrifty people, with a very
large proportion of Scotch blood in their veins, and are
mostly Catholics. We enjoyed immensely the picture
of the village as seen from the yacht, and had more
than one occasion to note the genial hospitality, the
general good-humor, the unaffected modesty, and refreshing simplicity and honesty of the inhabitants.

CHAPTER VIII.

SCENERY AND FLY-MAKING.

"A brother of the angle must always be sped
    With three black palmers, and also three red;
    And all made with hackles."
                                    BARKER.

"Enwrapt I gaze with strange delight,
    While consciousnesses, not to be disowned,
    Here only serve a feeling to invite
    That lifts the spirit to a calmer height,
    And makes this rural stillness more profound."
                                    WORDSWORTH.

RULOFF succeeded in getting a couple of wagons, the owner of which agreed to land us on the banks of the swift-flowing Margaree before dark. How it was to be done, I could not conjecture; but at that time I was not acquainted with the Cape Breton horse or the Cape Breton driver. In the two-horse team we put most of our innumerable traps, such as blankets, tents, rods, guns, and the et cetera of a fisherman's outfit. These were safely and snugly bestowed under the seats, while on them were the entire company, except Fletcher and myself, who took the dog with us in a single team drawn by a very sorry-looking horse.

"Come, gentlemen, it is time to be off," cried the driver. "Are you ready?"

"Ready!" was the response from both wagons.

"Then git up!" and crack went the whip, and away sped the horses, so suddenly that our heads were driven back from our shoulders to an angle of forty-five degrees, and we involuntarily cried, "Ugh!" in the most approved Indian fashion, and held on to the seats with both hands.

Down the street we rushed, raising clouds of dust, and then beyond the confines of the village, when we laid our course for Mabou, seven miles distant. It was a very uneven road, in that it went up hill and down, but very smooth, in that it was well made and had no ruts. The views we had of the island landscapes every now and then made me wish that all my friends and a few of my enemies were there to enjoy them; for no man can hold enmity in his heart when he is gazing upon such ravishing scenes. At one time we drove for miles through the silent forest, the only sound to be heard being the shrill voice of the little chipmunk, or the dull thud of the woodpecker's bill on the bark of a tree. The only game we saw was a covey or two of partridges—a most remarkable bird for one or two peculiarities—and a score or so of rabbits. I dislike to fire at a rabbit, for, unless you kill him outright, he makes you feel as though you were committing a murder. If you happen to simply wound him, he utters a cry not unlike that of a sick infant, and as you rap him on the head to end his misery, you seem to yourself a kind of ogre who is gathering children for an evening meal. The partridge, on the other hand, is so thoroughly stupid, especially in places where he is not often shot at, that you draw a bead on him without the slightest remorse. We ran across half a dozen pecking away on the side of the road, and fired at the farthest one first. If we had fired at the first one, some of the shot would have passed over him and frightened the others. They do not care for noise, and are not at all disturbed unless they are personally interfered with; so we successively shot the first, then the next, then the next, and so on, until we got to the last fellow, who, coming to the conclusion that something was wrong, put for the underbrush, where it was impossible to follow. I have again and again shot three partridges off the same tree, doing it in the most deliberate manner. If you kill the one on the topmost branch, he will in dropping frighten the others; but if you shoot the one nearest the ground first, you may reload at your leisure and bag the others.

At another time we drove along a high ridge, with a long stretch of land lying at our feet on the right, dotted here and there with a farm-house, while the broad, smooth, deep-blue waters of the gulf stretched to the horizon on the left. It was a scene for a painter, and I can not tell you how sorry I felt that I had neglected to bring with me a photographic apparatus with which to reproduce the panorama for home use and pleasure. It is so easy to learn enough of the mystic art of photography to obtain reminders of one's journeyings, that the camera has become one of the indispensables of a traveler's luggage.

Mabou is a lovely creek, making inland from the coast for several miles, and into which the Mabou

River pours its treasures. There were no trout there, however, since the thrifty inhabitants had erected just above its mouth a huge saw-mill, whose dust filled the water and choked the fish. And, by the way, these saw-mills are to be found on a vast number of streams, rendering them almost entirely useless for fishing purposes. The troublesome and often fatal saw-dust gets into the gills of the trout, and after a time depopulates the river. We saw in the Mabou many a shady nook overhung by branches—a capital home for the trout—and were almost inclined to joint our rods and fix our reels and flies; but on the bottom lay a couple of inches of sawdust, and we were informed that no fish were there.

At the head of the creek, just over the bridge, on the side of a couple of steep hills, the higher piled on top of the lower, sits the little village of Mabou. It has forty or fifty houses, a post-office, a blacksmith-shop, a notion store, where calico and molasses are sold indiscriminately, but no church. It is a rather neat, but an awfully slow place. There seems to be plenty of oxygen in the air, but the people are nevertheless sluggish and careless to the last degree. They gathered about our wagons while we went into the store for cheese, crackers, and poor cigars, but were not lively enough to ask questions. A Yankee would have known the biography of each separate individual of the party in five minutes; but strangers we entered the village, and strangers we left it.

By this time the dog—fearful reminiscence—began to set up sundry howlings, which rendered our trip unpleasant, and made even life itself seem less desirable.

He would thrust his head over the dash-board, and bark at those in the head wagon, until it seemed to me that a fatal bronchitis must make short work with him. But his throat was of leather, and his lungs of brass. He barked, howled, moaned incessantly, what for I did not know, nor have I yet found out. I whipped him and coaxed him by turns, but to no purpose. It seemed as though his interior were a cave of the winds, and that his mouth was a trumpet through which they unceasingly surged. At last, tired out, we let him go, and he bolted for the next thirty miles up hill and down, until the pads on his fore-feet were worn through; still, when he dropped on the side of the road from sheer exhaustion, and we lifted him into the wagon again, he renewed the same unnatural howlings, which made us feel, as a young mother does when her baby cries, that there must be a pin sticking into it somewhere which she can not find.

Beyond Mabou through the same delightful scenery we passed, with here a view of the land, and there a refreshing sight of the sea, until we reached Broad Cove, another little village at the cross-roads, and so on until night fell, and found us still six miles from the Margaree. By this time the horses were tired, and slackened their speed. The driver, however, cheered them on with the potent encouragement of his whip-lash, until from the head wagon came the welcome words—

" Here we are, and there is the river !"

The first part of the statement we readily agreed to, but as to the river, nothing could be seen but a hazy fog, of serpentine shape, that stretched itself along the valley.

" Under that fog the river, and in that river the sal-mon !" cried Bertric.

We were too tired to respond to the sentiment with *éclat;* for we had been sitting in one position, and that a cramped and uncomfortable one, for seven hours, had had nothing to eat but hard bread, and cheese which would have passed for shoe-leather if it had been tan-ned, and felt in no mood to be hilarious.

It was too late to set up our tents, so we tried for a lodging at a small house not far off.

" Could you take us in for the night ?" inquired Ru-loff, with an imploring look that would have given him a verdict before any jury.

The owner of the house, which was a single-story affair, looked at us, seven in number, and said slowly, but with ominous decisiveness,

"Couldn't think of it."

" But, my friend, what can we do ?" said Algar.

" Don't know," replied the proprietor of the estate.

" Why can't you take us in ?" meekly asked Stigand.

" 'Cause house full now; wife sick; not a bed in house ; only floor to sleep on, and can't have you there. So now."

That ended the matter as effectually as though the Fates had spoken.

" I'll find you a place," said Nimrod, cheeringly. " Follow me."

So we trudged behind him for three quarters of a mile, and at last, at about ten o'clock, saw quite a mod-ern-looking house on the hill-top. A knock at the door, and a gruff voice asked,

" Wha' ye want ?"

"Want to get in," said three of us at once, by a kind
of instinct, and as though to give emphasis to the re-
quest.

"Weel, wait a bit, and I'll undo the door."

The door was unbarred, and a hale, hearty old
Scotchman presented himself, and bade us welcome to
his homestead. He even roused the family from their
slumbers, and got us a supper of bread and milk.

When the time came to retire—and that time was
immediately after supper—our host entered the room
where we were sitting, and said,

"I hae ony won bed."

"Well, no matter; we'll sleep on the floor," we said;
and with that we spread out our shawls and the wolf-
skin.

"I understand there is a clergymon among ye," he
continued.

"Humph!" I said, "is that so? Well, he is no better than the rest of us, and must take his chances."

"Not so; an' I will not hear ye say it, young mon,"
responded our host. "The clergymon must hae the
bed."

I remonstrated, but to no purpose. The bed I must
have, and the bed I did have. There was a short,
sharp controversy over the matter, which ended, as
usual, in an unconditional surrender on my part.

"Call me early, mother, dear," were our last words
uttered; "call me early, for we want a salmon for
breakfast," and then we fell asleep.

Oh! the delights of a dreamless sleep after a weary
day. It is more than tired nature's sweet restorer—it is
the shadowy and silent vale through which one passes

to a re-creation of body and mind. What a delicious sense of relief creeps over you as you throw yourself full length on the couch, and relax every muscle, giving yourself up to that misty, hazy something which covers the world, and makes it grow dimmer and dimmer to the sight, until it is lost to view entirely.

I had not slept five minutes, apparently, before I heard the hoarse voice of Nimrod in my ear:

" Four o'clock, sir, and a fine morning."

I shook myself to get hold of my whereabouts, and then, remembering the salmon river, dressed as quickly as possible. It was July, but there was thick frost on the window-panes, while the grass looked as though it had been snowing in the night.

Let me walk slowly through my narrative now, for there is an exquisite pleasure connected with every detail of salmon-fishing. It is unlike any thing else in the world; and he who has never played with a fifteen-pounder of this species, knowing that he holds his prey only by the uncertain tenure of a single piece of silk-worm gut, has yet to enjoy one of the most fascinating and exciting experiences of life.

First, my rod. It has three joints, and is seventeen feet six inches and a half long—of course, a double-handed rod. In all the seventeen feet and six inches there is no one spot where it yields any more than it does at any other spot. From tip to butt it springs evenly. The first joint is of greenheart, whose fibres lie side by side in the snuggest and most friendly fashion; the second is of lance-wood, and the third of split bamboo. I always carry a spare tip, but have never had occasion to use it.

G

Secondly, my reel. This is a large-sized click reel, with rubber sides. The metal sides make the reel bungling and heavy. The click is not very strong, so the line passes over it with perfect freedom. Some fishermen prefer the multiplying reel, but I have always found it a nuisance, and very treacherous. It will do very well for trout, but is worse than useless for salmon. When the fish runs, he is apt to overhaul the line, at which critical moment the whole thing is in a snarl, from which you can extricate it, to be sure, if the fish will wait for you to do so; but, unfortunately, salmon, tides, and time never wait for any man. In that single moment of distress the fish is sure to make a plunge, and carry away with him ten or a dozen fathoms of your line. The simpler your gear when you are playing this prince of all the finny tribe the better. Your chances of bringing the fish to gaff depend upon the exquisite harmony between rod, line, reel, and fisherman.

Thirdly, my line. This consists of about one hundred yards of oiled silk. The best lines are like a whip-lash, bulky in the middle and tapering toward each end. This gives you weight enough to enable you to throw your fly into a pool three feet in width and fifty yards away, and let it touch the water as gently as though a moth had just dropped on its surface.

Fourthly, my casting-line. This is about eight feet long, and of picked gut. The first three feet, those nearest the silk line, may be of three strands, very carefully twisted; the next three feet ought to be of two strands, while the last two feet should be of stout single gut.

Lastly, my flies. Let me here give you one warning : never make your own flies. It is cheaper and better to buy them—if you want to catch fish. Every fisherman ought to know enough to mend a fly when it gets torn, for it sometimes happens that a given combination of colors, for some unknown reason, will be very killing, while another fly, to all appearance very like it, will fail to attract a fish ; but it is not profitable on the whole to manufacture flies yourself. Every one to his business, and let the fly-maker have a fair chance, is my motto.

I have never yet been able to tell why a salmon, who is a kind of chivalrous gentleman, a man of brains among fish, should be deceived and taken by a wretched counterfeit upon, indeed a burlesque of nature, called a fly. The things which are made in shops look no more like the real winged insects upon which the fish feeds than a rainbow looks like a dull gray cloud. It is pretty evident to my mind that the success of an artificial fly does not depend in any degree upon its having the general contour of a bug or natural fly, but upon a certain attractive combination of colors. I have caught trout, certainly, and they are younger members of the salmon family, with a fly which any living thing would blush to look like. The shape seems to have nothing to do with its killing quality, and the colors used may not be likened unto any thing in heaven above or the earth beneath. If you can catch the fish's eye, you catch the fish. I have tried the various, and in some cases commendable imitations of the house-fly and the gadfly and the moth of which the market is full, but I never had any success with them.

A common brown hackle is worth all the gutta-percha flies that were ever made. Again, in July and August, when the black or white moth is abundant, I have known a trout to persistently refuse the same colors on my hook, though I dropped the fly over his head as noiselessly as a shadow, yet a few minutes after he has risen, with a rush that took him clean out of water, at a little fiery-brown feather, the like of which he never saw before.

A young fly-fisherman is almost always under the delusion that he must needs purchase an enormous assortment of flies, of all sizes and colors, and fills his book with a lot of expensive material which afterward proves to be absolutely useless. Some over-scientific sportsmen have laid down the rule that a different fly is necessary for every season of the year; but good Isaak Walton has disposed of this nonsense in the following paragraph, to which every practical fisherman will give his assent:

"That whereas it is said by many that in fly-fishing for a trout, the angler must observe his twelve several flies for the twelve months of the year; I say, he that follows that rule, shall be as sure to catch fish, and be as wise, as he that makes hay by the fair days in an Almanac, and no surer."

This is far better advice than the following, which is as poor in sense as in poetical mint:

> "A brown-red fly at morning gray,
> A darker dun in clearer day;
> When summer rains have swelled the flood,
> The hackle red and worm are good.
> At eve, when twilight shades prevail,
> Try the hackle white and snail."

But here follow two lines, the admonition in which it is necessary to observe:

"Be mindful aye your fly to throw,
Light as falls the flaky snow."

And yet, important as this warning is, I do not think it necessary, in American waters at least, to throw with the accuracy which is demanded by another sportsman in these words: "No one is fairly entitled to be called an artist who can not readily throw his fly into a pint-pot at eighteen yards." In order to be an accomplished fisherman, one need not be such a gifted artist as this, though he ought to be able to cast his trout-fly a distance of twenty yards even with tolerable accuracy, and to throw his salmon-fly well across a stream that is twenty-five or thirty yards wide in a calm day. If he can accomplish either of these exploits, he is ready for the work.

There is one method of throwing the fly to which we have not given sufficient attention, however, and the value of which we have not properly estimated. Nearly all our streams are lined with underbrush, and nothing is more fretful than to get your hook and casting-line entangled in sundry branches just over the fish's head. You may pull, but to no purpose, for the point of the hook is fast in the wood; you may utter expletives which make the leaves turn yellow as in autumn, but these have no effect on the snarl. There are only two things to be done—you may wade across the stream, and thus frighten the fish from his covert, or you may part your line. In either case you have suffered a misfortune, and lost your temper.

What is called the underthrow obviates all this.   If you are skilled in it, you can throw twenty yards right under the branches of overhanging trees, and not touch a trap.   Pritchard, who is an adept in this science, taught me, and it has saved me many a moment of supreme embarrassment.   You cast your fly ahead of you, say five or eight yards, letting it rest on the water, then reeling off five or six yards more of slack line, by a quick motion from left to right or from right to left, you throw the slack ahead with force enough to draw the fly after it, and it lands at the required spot with a gentle snap like that of a whip-lash.

As for the time when to fish, there is but one rule, and that is to fish whenever you feel like it.   There are so many whims about cloudy days and sunny days and windy days, that if you attended to all the warnings that have been given you would never bring a fish to net.

One old saw runs thus:

" When the wind is south,
It blows your bait into the fish's mouth ;"

but Solomon, who himself indulged in the innocent sport of angling, says of another pursuit, " He that considers the wind shall never sow," intimating pretty plainly that if you want to sow, and have any seed to sow withal, you may sow it and be done with it, whether the wind blows or not.   The same is true of angling. Fish are certainly capricious, but there is no rule by which they are whimsical, and the only sensible thing to do is to go a-fishing whenever you wish to, and take the luck that comes in a philosophical spirit.

Now that I have quoted Scripture, I ought to be allowed to say that the pleasures of angling were not entirely unknown to the sages and prophets. Solomon says that " his beloved had eyes like the fish-pools of Heshbon," which shows plainly enough that he had visited those pools. It is less than probable that he visited them simply to note their natural beauty, or to watch the finny tribe at their play, and much more than probable that he was accustomed to drop a line and try his luck.

It is evident that in the earliest times the various means of catching fish which are in use to-day were known. Job asks, " Canst thou fill his skin with barbed irons? or his head with fish-spears?" Those same barbed irons and fish-spears are to be found on every fisherman that sails out of Gloucester Harbor, and they are used for the same purpose and in the same way as in the olden time, and, if I mistake not, I have lately seen harpoons, with which fin-backs and sword-fish are taken, old-fashioned enough to have been the property of some sturdy Hebrew of three thousand years ago.

Isaiah says, " The fishers shall mourn, and all they that cast angle upon the brooks shall lament, and they that spread nets upon the waters shall languish." Habakkuk adds, " They take up all of them with the angle, they catch them in their net, and gather them in their drag."

But to go back to fly-making, for I take it that the science of angling needs no defense from me. Some of the best and greatest men who have ever lived have been fishermen, and those who were not would have been had the opportunity presented. The angler's oc-

cupation induces introspection, reverie, and reflection.
He gets *en rapport* with nature, and becomes refreshed
in his inner being. The true angler is always an honest, courteous, mild-mannered gentleman. He sits on
the banks of the stream so quietly, and so delightfully
absorbed in contemplation, that the friendly spider
mistakes his broad shoulders for a brown rock, and
stretches his web from it to the nearest tree. It is
certainly a life of innocent pleasure without an atom
of alloy.

Still, never make your own flies. I have had a deal
of experience in that direction, which has taught me to
pay Pritchard four dollars a dozen rather than make
them at a cost of fifty cents. Some time ago I was an
enthusiast about home-made flies, but my enthusiasm
has oozed away, and I have no wish to recall it.

I literally followed the advice of Gay:

> "To frame the little animal, provide
> All the gay hues that wait on female pride;
> Let nature guide thee. Sometimes, golden wire
> The shining bellies of the fly require;
> The peacock's plumes thy tackle must not fail,
> Nor the dear purchase of the sable's tail.
> Each gaudy bird some slender tribute brings,
> And lends the growing insect proper wings:
> Silks of all colors must their aid impart,
> And every fur promote the fisher's art."

With all these several materials, and many more,
had I provided myself, and with a very hopeful heart I
set about the task. I soon found, however, that my
fingers were too large for the business, and that the
cunning skill, which deftly joins part to part and leaves
no ragged chasm between, was wanting. I must con-

fess that my first attempt was so far distant from my
ideal that the length of the journey to perfection in
the art was exceedingly discouraging. The dubbing
of hog's hair would not lie smooth ; the tinsel, whose
glittering spirals are supposed to be especially fascinating, would insist upon uncoiling itself just as I was
about to fasten it ; the tail would get awry, or come
out altogether and drop on the floor ; the head was a
bulbous nodule of worsted which was unpleasantly suggestive of hydrocephalus; and the wings—ah! they
were my despair; they would not stay where I put
them, and my fingers were so clumsy that the little fly
seemed like a cambric needle in the grip of a black-
smith's vise. However, I persevered until it was finished, and then, holding it up timidly for the exami-
nation and criticism of a friend who was reading at
my side, I asked,

" How do you like it ?"

" Broiled ; how do you ?" the hard-hearted fellow replied, without lifting his head from the book.

" But I have finished it, and want your opinion," I
persisted.

" I never did like fly-time," he responded, without
deigning to give me a look.

Not to be put off in this way, I insisted upon an expression of opinion by putting the fly on his book, and
saying,

" There, don't you think it pretty ?"

" Yes—pretty ugly," was the only response.

" Don't you think it well made for a first attempt ?"
I continued.

" Oh yes," he replied, not much interested in the

subject; " it is fearfully and wonderfully made. What can I say more?"

" But, really now, be serious for a moment, just for the sake of the surprise you will enjoy, and tell me what you think of it?" I continued.

" Well," he answered, " I think it looks as though it had been struck by a rainbow, and a piece of every color and shade had stuck to it."

" Don't you think a trout would take it?" I said, trying to get some little consolation from him.

" Oh, he might, if he was very hungry; but I shouldn't want to eat that kind of a fish."

" Dear me !" I moaned disconsolately, " what shall I do with it? I don't think I can make any thing better."

He replied, " Buy your flies, and put that into a . museum of monstrosities."

The advice was good, and I give it to you. Learn to mend your flies, but never take the trouble to make them. I have a couple of hundred which I have manu-factured during the last few years, but when I go into the woods I always lift out the tray that contains them with a sigh, and then put a couple of dozen of Pritchard's best into my book for use.

CHAPTER IX.

A SALMON AND A FOX.

"A whirr ! a whirr ! the salmon's out
Far on the rushing river.
Hark to the music of the reel !
The fitful and the grating ;
It pants along the breathless wheel,
Now hurried, now abating."
STODDART.

" The little foxes that spoil the vines."
SOLOMON.

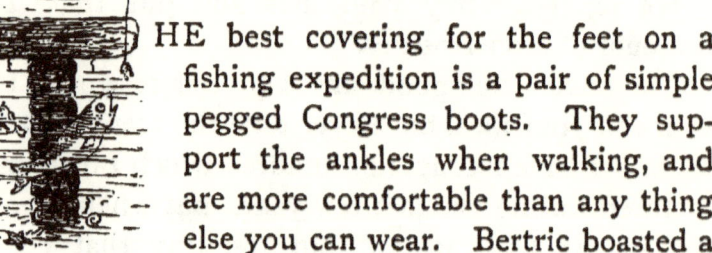 HE best covering for the feet on a fishing expedition is a pair of simple pegged Congress boots. They support the ankles when walking, and are more comfortable than any thing else you can wear. Bertric boasted a pair of patent rubber boots reaching up to the waist. They were not very heavy—on the contrary, they were wonderfully light ; but if you happen, as you are likely to do, to step on a sharp stone or hit against a snag half-way up the leg, you are compelled thereafter to carry about with you a gallon or two of water ; and if, disgusted at this proceeding, you lie down on your back and lift your leg, under the delusion that the water will run out, the precious liquid, which has a way of doing things all its own, will pour itself down

your back and drench you.   There is nothing neater,
or on the whole more comfortable, than Congress
shoes.   To be sure, you get your feet wet, but no man
has any right to claim the honorable distinction of
fisherman who is afraid of wet feet.

Now then, we are all ready at 4.15 A.M. to start.
There is a chill in the air which reminds you of November, and the grass is as wet as though the flood
had just ebbed; but these are slight drawbacks.   You
munch your cracker and cheese as you wind your way
to the banks of the river half a mile off, and are su-
premely happy.   The birds twitter their matins, the
sun is just climbing the hill, the farmers are all asleep,
and you are whistling or singing.

Here at last lies the noble Margaree at our feet.   It
is altogether a remarkable stream, and one of the few
in which every body has a right to fish.   Last month
half a dozen English officers encamped in that hut opposite, and in a week killed fifteen salmon ranging
from ten pounds to twenty-one.   Two others are there
now; but pray don't speak to them, except to say Good-
morning, for they will surely tell you there are no fish
here.   Their motto is, two lines are better than four.
How beautifully the river winds among the hills! but
just where we stand, and for a couple of miles, there is
not even a bush on the bank.   No fear of tangling your
line here.   The stream is about seventy-five feet wide,
and that enables us to stand on either bank and whip
every pool.

" Well, Nimrod, what is the prospect ?"

" Good, sir; good, sir; I have caught salmon in this
river weighing forty pound with a single gut "—(that

I suspect is not true)—" and I hope you may have as good luck."

" Are there any trout here ?"

" Trout ?   The only fear is that they will snap at your fly, and not give the salmon a fair chance."

(That, too, I suspected to be an exaggeration.)

" Good enough !   Just put my rod together.   Here, Stigand, give me that reel, will you, and we will see whether by any mischance Nimrod can tell the truth."

" But there is not a pool in sight — it is all shoal water," said Bertric.

" Never you mind," responded Nimrod, somewhat touched; " there are pools enough within twenty rods of us."

The rod is all right, the reel is firmly fixed, the casting-line is a good one, the tail fly is white and brown, and there is nothing left except to find the fish.

" Here is a trout !" cried Bertric, as he killed and brought to creel a speckled beauty of about a pound weight.

" And here's another !" cried Stigand, as he made fast to a plucky fellow somewhat larger.

" Let out your line and play him !" yelled Nimrod, " or you will lose him.   That's a white trout just from salt water.   Handle him tenderly."

The warning was well-timed.   The fish ran out nearly twenty yards of line, and then gave a leap about three feet from the water, which tumbled from his silver sides in glistening drops.   He was a noble fellow, and not until after ten minutes of skillful and patient play was he landed.   He weighed a pound and a half.

" This is rich sport!" cried Bertric, who jerked a little too quickly, and drew the fly from his second fish's jaws—" Ah! he's gone. Well, my beauty, just strike that fly once more, and I will give you a new sensation."

While the gentlemen were filling their creels with white and speckled trout, I went on about ten rods to watch Fletch catch his first fish with a fly. I envied the boy the rich experience which he was about to enjoy. He had carefully practiced the throw, and was ready for the capture.

" There's a good place, Fletch "—the salmon grounds were farther on. " Just drop your hackle over there, and see what will come of it."

The feather had no sooner touched the water than I saw a swirl, then heard a splash, and the fish was gone. He had overleaped. It would have done your heart good to see Fletch's eyes. They fairly stood out from his head, and flashed like two camp-fires. His cheeks were flushed, and altogether he looked remarkably handsome as he stood there intensely excited, disappointed, and chagrined.

" No matter, try once more," I said. But the wary fish wouldn't bite. He had seen the line, and quietly retired.

" Hold a minute, and we'll fix him," said Nimrod. " Let him rest for a while, and I will change your fly."

The book was forthcoming, and a fly with red body and tinsel and dark wings was tied on.

" There, throw carefully; let nothing but the fly touch the water, and you'll get him."

Sure enough. The feathered deceit had no sooner touched the surface than there came another rush, and this time with better aim, for the hook was fast in the trout's mouth. He broke at once for deeper water up stream. Whiz! went the line off the reel, while Fletch, keeping a taut hold on him, followed as fast as he could scamper. Once he tumbled into a hole and fell his length, but he soon scrambled to his feet again, and found to his great joy that the fish was still safe.

"Look out for that log; if he gets under it, then good-bye."

"Oh! I can't lose him—I mustn't lose him—I won't lose him," Fletch jerked out as he hurried on. With a slight strain on the line, the trout was guided into safe water, and after a while brought to land. He fought well and long, and was a prize worth having.

As I wandered off with Nimrod to the salmon grounds, I could not help regretting that the boy in all his life might not have just such another experience, and I envy any man the delicious excitement of catching his first heavy trout.

After we had followed the bank for a while I said to Nimrod,

"Look over there, man. Isn't that a princely palace for a fish to live in?" It was a pool about seven feet deep, and nearly twelve feet across. "Now, if there are any salmon in this river, one of them is sure to be in that spot."

I threw my line with all the skill I possessed, but there was no rise. This was a terrible disappointment, and a greater damper than I cared to confess, because, if a salmon takes at all, he generally takes at once. I threw again, and this time hauled out a little speckled trout weighing about six ounces.

" Throw him back, and let him grow," I said to Nimrod, as he unhooked him.

" No need of a gaff for him," he replied, as he threw him fifty feet up stream.

That was a specimen of my luck for the next hour. I whipped pool after pool, in each of which a salmon would have delighted to dwell, but with no success. A few insignificant trout were the only reward of my pains and labors — for it is no small task to wield a long salmon rod for that length of time; it is far more tiresome than one suspects who is not accustomed to the work. I lay down on some logs to rest for a bit, while Nimrod went ahead to prospect. I had been lying there perhaps ten minutes when I heard him crying out,

"Come here! come here!"

I was on my feet in an instant, and in a few seconds more was at his side.

" Well, what is it ?"

" I saw over there, near the bank, the swirl of a big fellow."

" Nimrod, you are fibbing, as usual," I said. " You always see swirls when I am not round, and you catch your biggest fish when you talk about them. I don't believe a salmon has flipped his tail in these waters for thirty days. There's my rod; let me see you catch this ghostly monster of your imagination."

He took the rod, and threw the fly with a masterly hand. It touched the water; and then I had a feeling that the stream was suddenly boiling, or that an infant earthquake was playing with the bottom. A splendid fellow, weighing fully ten or twelve pounds, threw himself half out of water, and unfortunately fell on the fly. No man could catch him under these circumstances, but the hook just pricked him as Nimrod jerked the line in—*O, me miserum,* but it was a sad sight, and a great calamity.

Nimrod stood looking at me with a sadness in his face which well becomes a fisherman under such trying circumstances, and for a while uttered no word. It was worse than useless to try again. That fish had learned too much, and would keep very still and be very wary for the rest of the day.

"Did you ever?" slowly muttered Nimrod, with a long, mournful interval between the words.

"No, I never," I replied, in a tone equally dolorous; and that is the entire conversation we had on the subject.

Matters were not to end thus, however. About an hour afterward I saw on a pool just ahead of me some wrinkles which made my cheeks turn red and my heart bound with hope. I crept as cautiously as I could to the proper point, looked at my fly, saw that the line was clear, and then made a cast. I really believe that fly never touched water, for the hungry fish took him on the wing. A quick jerk, and the hook was well fastened in his jaws. Now for a tussle!

I think the fish was taken by surprise. He lay perfectly still in the water long enough for me to reel in the slack, and feel of him, when, comprehending the situation, he took for his motto, "Liberty or Death," and made a bold strike for the former. He was headed up stream, and the way he traveled was a marvel. The line went whistling from the reel, until there were only ten or fifteen yards left, while I tried in vain to stay his progress by compelling him to keep the rod bent. There was no tire-out to him. I saw that I should lose him if I didn't run, so I ran as fast as I could, leaping over dead logs and jumping across holes until I was tired enough to drop in my tracks. Then the salmon took a notion to sulk. He lay at the bottom of the river long enough for me to reel in about seventy yards of line, and then apparently determined to sulk my patience all away.

I gave him one or two steady pulls, but I might as well have pulled against a rock. He seemed to have grown to the bottom, and to have become a part of it.

"I say, Nimrod, throw a stone in, and mind you don't cut my line."

"That will I," he replied, and thereupon the stone struck the water and sank. There was a slight motion in response, but nothing more.

"Give him another, and a bigger one." This was done, but the stone went so close to the line that I feared for a moment I had lost my fish. He was all right, however, and immediately started for a trip down stream. I followed him as best I could, but he went more rapidly than my legs could carry me. By this time I had been fast to him just twenty minutes, and was so tired that I determined to run the risk and give him the butt. The rod bent to the task in the most loving way, and the salmon began to grow palpably tired. I managed by dint of good-luck to keep him clear of a sharp rock in the middle of the river, and to guide him into a pool on the nearer side of the bank, and directly opposite the one where he had struck. He was resting for a great struggle, when I said to Nimrod,

"Can't you wade in and gaff him? I can't hold on much longer."

"Just you keep steady, sir, and I'll do my best."

He walked into the river very cautiously up to his knees, then up to his waist, when, bending forward, he found he could just reach him.

"Now then, steady!" he said, while I stood as rigid as a statue, the rod well bent and the line taut. I saw the shining point of the gaff under his belly, and the quick backward motion of Nimrod's arm. Then came a struggle, a splash, and a victory.

"I've got him!" said Nimrod.

"Good!" I replied; "land him with great care." Then he was laid gently on the grass, his scaly sides glistening like molten silver, while I enjoyed a certain sensation of pride which only he can feel who plays an eighteen-pounder with a single gut and brings him to gaff.

Curiously enough, I did not get another stir, though I whipped the stream until noon. I had had sport enough, however, and felt content with the day's work. The truth is, there are very few delicious sensations in life entirely unalloyed with pain, and playing a salmon successfully is one of them. He is

> A fish of wonderful beauty and force,
> That bites like a steel-trap, and pulls like a horse;

and a man grows taller of stature and broader of heart

when he has safely landed one of these glories of the deep, after an hour's strategy and struggle.

Pray do not think me over-enthusiastic. I am not so fascinated by the gentle art as to say that

> "All pleasures but the angler's bring
> I' th' tail repentance like a sting;"

but I do delight in the change from the worrying troubles of city life to the sweet and refreshing silence of the woods.

> "I love to see the man of care
>   Take pleasure in a toy;
> I love to see him row or ride,
>   And tread the grass with joy,
> Or throw the circling salmon-fly
>   As lusty as a boy.
>
> "The road of life is hard enough,
>   Bestrewn with slag and thorn;
> I would not mock the simplest joy
>   That made it less forlorn,
> But fill its evening path with flowers
>   As fresh as those of morn."

We soon after came across the other gentlemen of the party, who had enjoyed excellent luck, killing some very fine silver trout, and a dozen or so of the brook trout, weighing all the way from three quarters of a pound to a pound and a half. By this time, having come off without any breakfast, we were tolerably hungry. Fletch was so completely famished that, while we were busy putting our rods in order and admiring the beauties who had rewarded us for our toil, he built a fire out of drift-wood, and with a pronged stick to hold the fish steady managed to cook one of the smaller trout. He was compelled to eat it without bread, pepper, or salt, or salt pork either—that ambrosial mystery with which trout should always be cooked; and the consequence was that, though the first few mouthfuls were delicious, the next few were only tolerable, and the next still hardly palatable, until at length he laid the charred remains on the grass, and expressed a preference for a different style of cooking.

Bertric, who was always saying bright things, threw his hands up as though he had hit upon some new discovery, and said,

"Fellows, there's a farm-house yonder, and in that farm-house milk and bread, and in our wallets is silver, the logical result of all which is—the very thought revives me—dinner!"

We were all hilarious except Nimrod, who was glum. That was a bad sign.

"Well, Ancient Mariner," said Bertric, with a sly hit in the intercostal regions of Nimrod, "prythee, why so sad?"

Nimrod looked up with a shadow on his face, and replied,

"Because that man don't keep a cow."

"There goes my dinner!" cried Bertric:

> "''Twas ever thus, from childhood's hour
> I've seen my fondest hopes decay.'"

"Oh, no; you needn't despair, for Jessie has cream," said Nimrod.

"Jessie?—who is Jessie?" cried we all at once.

"No matter who, nor yet what she is," some one said; "if she has cream, it is enough."

We afterward found it not only enough, but too

much. A walk—no, it was not that, for the word walk
has a spring, an elasticity of suggestion in it—rather
a trudge, for that is a heavy, leaden word, which expresses our condition—of half an hour, and we saw on
a hill-side, the roots of whose ancient trees had never
been taken out, a—what shall I call it? It was not a
house, for that expression gives you an idea of comfort
and cleanliness. It was a frame building, about fifteen
feet square, covered with a roof partly thatched, while
the rest of it was covered with slabs. It was sided
with castaway boards, which with singular unanimity
refused to lie close together. In the window, one of
the four squares had glass in it, but of the others two
had a tuft of grass and an old hat, while the third had
nothing. The door was hung on leathern hinges.
The floor was the original earth; the chimney and
fire-place were of mud, and for beds there were two
bunks, like those in a condemned fishing-sloop.

Nimrod stood in the midst of this wilderness of
squalor, and yelled " Jessie! Jessie!" at the top of his
voice; but no Jessie appeared. " I'll find the girl; she's
hiding," he said, and with that he rushed to the barn,
whence he soon emerged, bringing a woman apparently
forty years of age. She came with great hesitation and
diffidence, and only after repeated assertions on the
part of Nimrod that nobody would hurt her. He
had found her hidden away by crouching behind two
cows.

She was a pure-blooded Gaelic woman, speaking only
her native language, with an exceptional word every
now and then of very bad English. Her hair, which
was in the utmost conceivable disorder, partly tied in

a knot, and partly dangling over her shoulders, was coal-black. Her eyes resembled two lumps of burnished Lehigh. Her dress —if the few tattered articles which failed to conceal her person could be called by so respectable a name —consisted of a variety of remnants which had seen better days, but which under no circumstances could experience worse. We all thought of Stonehenge ; for  she was an ideal Druidess, and one of the "raal old stock." We should not have been more surprised if we had been suddenly transported to the time when Boadicea led her hosts through British forests. It was a superb touch of ancient history, not only in the person who stood before us, but in all the surroundings— the mud hut, the stumps of trees, the untilled ground, the background of forest, with not another domicile in sight to remind us of the nineteenth century.

One of the party sat on the only seat in the hut, which was a three-legged stool, and the others stood or occupied the door-step.

"Jessie, have you any cream ?" said Nimrod.

That much at least she comprehended. She quickly brought from an outhouse a large water-bucket full of such cream as my eyes had never beheld. Here was a good dinner, and our anticipations were of the most

favorable kind. But they were quickly dashed with
disappointment, for Jessie's subsequent proceedings
dispelled the illusion. She washed her hands and arms
in a vessel which had been recently used for cooking
purposes, then deliberately rinsed a couple of pint
bowls in the same water, and wiped them on a towel
whose condition was indescribable. And that was
household economy.

"Cream don't agree with me—it makes me sick,"
said Bertric.

"I don't feel as hungry as I did," said Stigand. "I
think I won't spoil my appetite until we get home."

This was a dilemma. I was dying for the cream, but
under the peculiar circumstances felt that at least the
edge of my appetite was gone. So, while the rest
were engaged in conversation, I took one of the bowls,
slipped out to a spring near by, washed it thoroughly,
and then came back triumphant. I dipped it into the
bucket, and had my fill. The others took the hint, and
did the same thing; so we had a very delicious meal
after all.

I speak of this experience because of the central personage. You do come across in these far-away coun-
tries, once in a while, a most imposing bit of ancient
time. As in some secluded alcove of a museum you
surprise yourself with the sight of a rare antique, the
last trace of which you supposed lost, so in Cape Breton, and along the upper edges of Canada, you hit
upon a human curiosity at rare intervals who reminds
you of the time when the world was in its swaddling-
clothes. Jessie looked like, and I think even now that
she may have been, one of the original Iceni who help-

ed to throw up the earthworks at Devil's Ditch, to keep the Romans out. As a fly in amber, so she exists in the nineteenth century. I left her feeling that I had communed with the past, and with the hope that I might never see it again.

After dinner at the Scotchman's, some one of the party suggested that a good square meal cooked by Ah Boo would be very desirable. The truth is, we were half starved. The bread was sour and black, the coffee had not the most distant connection with either Java or Mocha, but was a drink by itself, while the tea was so decidedly "yarby" that we threw it out of the window when the maid turned her back. I can rough it in camp where I can cook myself, or oversee it; but the food which is found in the backwoods of Cape Breton would put to a severe test the digestive organs of a bronze lion.

"Home it is!" we cried all at once, and in half an hour we had made arrangements with our host to carry us back in his two teams, and were on our way singing at the top of our voices at the prospect of a clean table-cloth. Thus perfectly does man's stomach rule and decide his destiny. The going and coming had cost each of the seven just seven dollars and sixty-nine cents in gold, and the net result was one salmon and a few trout. That is hardly a fair estimate, however, since we had enjoyed the scenery amazingly, and would not have missed the insight we got into the habits of the people, and the view of the Gaelic Jessie, for double the amount.

We went back by the same road along which we came, because there was no other. Nothing disturbed

H

the serenity of the trip until we reached Broad Cove, after which time my happiness at least was seriously marred. One of the horses had lost a shoe, so we had twenty minutes for refreshments. Bertric went to one house, where they had milk but no bread, and to another, where they had bread but no milk. We succeeded in making a combination of the two homesteads, and were about to leave, when a farmer's wife called out after us, saying she had a tame fox, and wanting to know if we would like to see it.

Of course we were eager to gaze on any thing in the way of a curiosity, and so we filed Indian fashion through a narrow gate and into the back-yard. Little Reynard was a red-haired beauty, and my heart warmed to him to such an extent that I boldly asked the price. The woman agreed to let me have him for two dollars, if I would give her half a dollar for his chain. As a fox without a chain is a great deal closer to the woods than he is with one, I bought both, and for a minute was happy. My happiness began to curdle, however, in a short time, and not long afterward it turned irretrievably sour. Behold Fletch and myself in the single wagon. I had the fox in my lap, his chain wound around my arm. The dog was on the bottom of the wagon, howling with all his might, and so uneasy that I was compelled to hold on to his collar to keep him from jumping out, which would have increased our trouble, because he was so foot-sore that he could not run a rod. The horse required incessant urging of the most stimulating kind, which I administered at paroxysmal intervals with a long branch which I had cut for the occasion. Besides this, I had a gun

between my legs, which the restive dog came near fir-
ing several times by rubbing up against the hammer.
I never came nearer losing my temper, and giving up
the ghost altogether, than I did on that occasion.
Fletch could not help me, for he had the reins in one
hand, while with the other he guarded several bundles
which seemed inclined to leap over the back-board.
To make matters worse, and as though Fate had it all
her own way, and had determined to pile the Ossa on
the Pelion of vexation, one of the boards in the bottom
of the wagon dropped out, which let the dog half-way
through every once in a while. My time was chiefly
spent in whipping the horse and cosseting the fox,
catching hold of the gun just as it was about to drop
out of the wagon, and yanking the dog from the hole
through which he and the small-sized buffalo skin,
which served as a mat, were continually falling. My
conversation was somewhat fragmentary, and consisted
of ejaculatory phrases without any special coherence,
while my thoughts were directed from one subject to
another with such rapidity that my whole brain was
dizzy. "Get up there! Poor Foxy, you needn't be
frightened. Keep still, Frank!"—the dog. "There he
goes through that hole again!" I think I have seldom
in my life experienced such a sense of relief as I enjoyed when we finally drove down to the wharf and
hailed the *Nettie.*

When we got on board Ah Boo had a hot supper
ready, and a happier set of men your eyes never beheld.

CHAPTER X.

ALONG PRINCE EDWARD'S.

"The powerful sails, with steady breezes swell'd,
Swift and more swift the yielding bark impell'd."
FALCONER.

E intended to make up for loss of sleep on the Margaree expedition by lying idle all the next day. There is something delicious and recuperative in the indolence of yacht life. To lie down on deck, a thick wolf-skin underneath you, book in hand, and to skip the dry places in the narrative by lifting the eyes to the sea, forests, and sky occasionally, constitutes one of the most delightful of possible experiences. All this pleasure we had proposed to ourselves; but in the morning the wind came up fresh from the southwest, and Edwards suggested that it would be too bad to lose such a breeze.

Our plans were, however, in great confusion. We had hoped to go to the Bay of Islands on the west coast of Newfoundland, and Rev. Mr. Harvey, of St. John's, Newfoundland, had, with kindness unparalleled, engaged four Indians whom we were to take aboard at the Bay of Despair, and had also gathered a quantity of information for our use. But there were several reasons why it was impossible to change our hopes into realities. We gave this project up, for which we had made very extensive preparations, and had not yet fixed upon the new route to be taken. At some future time I hope I shall be able to carry out a plan which has been in my mind for a long time, namely, to cross the island of Newfoundland by way of the Bay of Islands, go up the Humber River in canoes, then by a short portage cross to Deer Lake, thence to Great Indian Pond, and so on down the River of Exploits to Hall's Bay. That is an ideal trip for a party of half a dozen sturdy and enduring men. In the woods are plenty of caribou, with once in a while a black bear for a target at one hundred yards. In the water are salmon in great abundance, and trout enough to fill the creeks of the world, and on the water mallards and canvas-backs.

It started my lachrymal fount, and gave me a very queer, dull, and unpleasant feeling about the heart, when I convinced myself that the project must be abandoned. But we were all disappointed in the progress we had made at night. During July and August the wind has a very disagreeable way of going down with the sun, and leaving you to roll about, heading toward every point of the compass until daybreak. It was a rare fortune for us to make even thirty or forty miles from eight o'clock in the evening until seven the next morning; and many a night we slipped backward on the current, the big sails slatting, and not a breath of wind. This inevitable delay cut our vacation down at least two weeks, and rendered it impossible to accomplish all we had laid out.

"Yes," I said to Edwards, "it's a splendid breeze, but where shall we go? What we are after is good hunting and fishing, and where shall we find these things? When we got to Halifax, they told us the rivers were fished to death, but that we should find all we wanted farther on. When we reached Canso, they said the waters had been whipped until the last fish had taken to the ocean, and the woods contained nothing bigger than woodpeckers. We have just come from the Margaree, and have been informed that all the officers in the British army have been before us, but that we can get game enough in the higher latitudes. We can go to Aspee Bay, round Cape North, but we shall probably meet the same fortune there. They will send us to Newfoundland, and the Newfoundlanders will send us to Labrador, and the Labradorians will send us to Greenland."

"Aspee Bay," said Edwards—"I'm no pilot there; but I can carry you to Gaspe Bay, on the other shore, and I think you will get all you want there."

"Gaspe—where is that?" said Ruloff.

"Just this side of the mouth of the St. Lawrence," responded Edwards; "and the whole coast is full of interest, while the scenery is magnificent."

"Hallo, there, Nimrod!" I shouted.

"Aye, aye, sir," was the reply from that important functionary.

"Have you ever been to Gaspe?"

"That have I sir, and many a time.'

"Are there any deer in the woods?"

"The woods are full of them, sir," asserted this arrant knave, who never once confessed to ignorance of any subject or place.

" Can we get any ducks there ?"

" Ducks ? my eyes, sir ! I was out there once when we killed ducks with clubs, they were so thick. We filled the boat till we were afraid it would sink, and then were fairly driven home by the flocks of them that insisted on being killed."

This we knew to be a yarn told in the interest of two dollars, gold, a day ; but as Edwards assured us that he had seen plenty of birds around Bonaventura, just this side of Gaspe, we concluded to turn our prow in that direction.

" Well, up with your anchor, Captain Comstock, and we'll go as far as this wind will carry us."

The sails were hoisted, the anchor weighed, and in half an hour we were out of Port Hood, and headed for East Point Light, on the S.E. end of Prince Edward's Island.

That was another white day in our calendar. No sooner had we got fairly out to sea than the wind freshened to a ten-knot breeze, and we went bowling along at the most exhilarating rate. We sighted East Point when we had been out little over an hour, and in another hour we had passed it, and laid our course along the edge of the island. We sailed almost due west, and most of the time within a mile of the shore.

As we passed one inlet after another, the history of this most delightful spot, cuddling in the southwest corner of the magnificent gulf, was brought to mind. Prince Edward's Island is about one hundred and forty miles long, if you follow the bend of the land, the northern line of which resembles the concave line of a new moon, while it is only about ninety-five miles from

East Point to North Point, if you go by water. It contains 1,360,000 acres of rich land, with hardly any rocks,
and the soil is red in color like that of New Jersey.
There are no mountains, and only a few hills of any
considerable height. The coast is very low, seldom
rising in its steepest bluff to more than a hundred
feet. It was discovered by the irrepressible Cabot,
who called it St. John's, on the 24th of June, 1497,
and it consequently belonged to Great Britain according to the rule of the early navigators, which Freneau
has put in the following distich:

> "For the time once was, to all be it known,
>   When all a man sailed by, or saw, was his own."

Cabot took possession of it immediately after his
discovery of Newfoundland, when he was on "the
starboard tack," and running for the Strait of Fronfac,
or Canso. The greedy French, however, were the first
actual possessors by pre-emption, and they annexed it
to New France, or Canada, afterward leasing it, together
with the Magdalen Islands, which are only about twenty
leagues distant to the northeast, to the Sieur Doublett,
who was a captain in the French navy, to be held as a
feudal tenure of the company of Miscou. After the
capture of Louisburg, however, it fell again into English hands, and there it has remained ever since.

It is almost wholly dissimilar to any land that lies
adjacent. Its soil is especially favorable to ordinary
products, and it may well be called the granary of the
northeast. The climate is something wonderful, being
neither so cold in winter nor so hot in summer as
Lower Canada, while it is entirely free from the innu-

merable fogs which slip over Cape Breton and Nova Scotia. It is said that the inhabitants very frequently reach one hundred years of age without ever suffering from serious illness. The air is dry and bracing, and no better project could be set on foot than to empty the hospitals of the world on these generous shores. The fell diseases with which we of the eastern coast are so afflicted, as consumption, for example, and intermittent fevers, are never known ; while nonagenarians and centenarians who are still able to do a fair day's work on the farm are met with at every turn. Indeed, it is an ideal spot for the invalid ; and the time is not far distant when that ghastly crowd that yearly goes to Florida to die will change their course, and go to Prince Edward's to live. I have often wondered at this American folly which prompts one who is in the last stages of consumption, or who has a serious difficulty with throat or lungs, to leave a comfortable home that he may roost on the branches of the Florida coast, at a cost of five or six dollars a day and nothing to eat.

I sometimes suspect that it is all a ruse of the doctors, who do not care to have a patient die on their hands, and who, therefore, advise a trip to the sunny South, which sounds well enough, but which is in reality a trip to the grave-yard. Florida is a Moloch who must be dethroned. He has an insatiable appetite, and is everlastingly demanding more ; and more he will have, so long as fashion holds control over life and death as now. When we wake from our delusion, we shall find that the dry, bracing, life-giving atmosphere of some favored spot like Prince Edward's is worth far more than the subtle poison of Florida, even if the camellias do blossom there in February, and the sun coaxes the mercury up to seventy-five. I do not care to sit in judgment on the opinion of a physician, but if I had a cross-grained uncle who was worth a million, and who had made a will in my favor; and if this aforesaid relation was coughing about the house all day, giving me as it were an anticipatory view of his fortune; and if, furthermore, I was possessed of a diabolical thirst of gain, I should coax him to go to Florida, and, taking his exact measure in feet and inches, should confide it to a neighboring undertaker before he started. But if, on the other hand, I wished to retain him a little longer amid these sublunary scenes, free from bronchitis and tubercles, I should pack him off for some such secluded spot as Prince Edward's, where the refreshing air and equal temperature would rebuild his shattered constitution.

I would like nothing better than to land at St. Peter's Bay, and with a couple of ponies raised from good English stock, for which the island has become famous, start on a trip over the entire island, hunting in its woods, fishing in its rivers and lakes, and stopping at the always hospitable farm-houses at night. With sweet bread, fresh milk and eggs, and rich cream, I think I could manage to survive for a month or two at least.

That was certainly superb sailing we had that day. Every stitch of canvas drew. We had up, besides the deck sails, consisting of mainsail, foresail, and jib, the main and fore gaff topsails, the flying jib, and the jib topsail. The *Nettie* fairly danced through the water.

The sea was smooth, for we were under the lee of the
island, and the yacht, heeling over until the waves
once in a while swashed aboard, cut the deep as though
she were chasing an enemy, or being chased by one.
The sun was out in a sky almost cloudless, and the
white-caps made the gulf look like a caldron of molten
silver. Once in a while a gust would come which
suggested the propriety of taking in the top-hamper,
when every part of the standing rigging seemed to
strain itself to the utmost to hold on, and when the
vibrating ropes made a music which the sailor delights
to hear more than the tuneful chords of the harp; and
then again the wind would settle down for half an hour
to a blow so steady that the high-water mark on the
lee side did not vary an inch.

We tried to find some poetry which would fitly
describe our situation and feelings, but most of the
poets who have written about the merry and the dangerous moods of salt water were landsmen, and would
have been too seasick in a gale to think of rhyming.
There is a vast deal of shoal-water poetry, which ex-
pends its music on gulf-weed, the sea-mew, drift-wood,
the coral grove, and the ebb and flow, but very little
that may be called deep-sea poetry, which portrays the
sterner temper of old Ocean when he chafes and storms
in a glorious burst of indignation. It is one thing to
sit on an overhanging cliff and imagine a plunging
vessel on a lee shore, and quite another thing to be on
board, and put the actual scene in rhythmic phrase.

There is, however, a grandeur in these lines of Ho-
mer which brings the earnestness of the sea before
you, as little modern poetry does, and makes you

almost feel the crisp wind, as it dashes the spray in your face:

> "There was his palace in the deep sea-water,
>   Shining with gold, and builded firm forever;
>   And there he yoked him his swift-footed horses
>   (Their hoofs are brazen, and their manes are golden),
>   With golden thongs; his golden goad he seizes;
>   He mounts upon his chariot, and doth fly;
>   Yea, drives he forth his steeds into the billows."

Then again Scott, though he knew so little of sea-water, gives us a taste of an eight-knot breeze in his song, which I have repeated so many times in the ear of half a gale:

> "Merrily, merrily bounds the bark,
>   She bounds before the gale;
> The mountain breeze from Ben-na-darch
>   Is joyous in her sail.

> "With fluttering sound, like laughter hoarse,
>   The cords and canvas strain;
> The waves, divided by her force,
>   In rippling eddies chase her course
>   As if they laugh'd again."

How many times has the sailor stood at the stern, and, looking on the wake of the vessel, laughed in his heart to see the trembling waves apparently rush after the vessel as though they would try to catch it; and the low murmuring sound of the waters gurgling about the rudder have seemed to rebuke the craft for its intrusion among the sportive waves.

> "Merrily, merrily bounds the bark,
>   O'er the broad ocean driven;
> Her path by Ronin's mountain dark,
>   The steerman's hand has given.

"Merrily, merrily goes the bark,
    On a breeze from the northward free;
So shoots through the morning sky the lark,
    Or the swan through the summer sea.

"Merrily, merrily goes the bark;
    Before the gale she bounds;
So flies the dolphin from the shark,
    Or the deer before the hounds."

Longfellow, in his exquisite little poem on "The Wreck of the *Hesperus*," gives us a life-like view of the gale on a lee shore, and must have drawn on his own experiences when he talked of

"The vessel in its strength;
She shuddered, and paused like a frightened steed,
Then leaped her cable's length."

Byron, who was exceedingly fond of the water, and enjoyed the ocean in its roughest moods, has left but one poem at all worthy of the theme, but that is so grand that one likes to read it on shipboard, when he is far out at sea, and never tires of the orchestral rhythm of the lines which seem to fill his soul to complete satisfaction.

The only sailor poet in our language who has ventured to describe the ocean in calm and storm is William Falconer. When a boy he was

"Forlorn of heart, and by severe decree
Condemned reluctant to the faithless sea."

For many years he was only a forecastle-hand, and then obtained a position as midshipman on board the *Royal George*. Every lover of the water reads his "Shipwreck" with pleasure and admiration, for his descriptions are not only exquisite, but true to the letter. Here is a picture which no one has excelled, and which brings a ship on the eve of starting vividly to view:

> "All hands unmoor! proclaims a boisterous cry;
> All hands unmoor! the cavern'd rocks reply:
> Roused from repose aloft the sailors swarm,
> And with their levers soon the windlass arm:
> The order given, upspringing with a bound,
> They fix the bars, and heave the windlass round;
> At every turn the clanging pauls resound;
> Uptorn reluctant from its oozy cave
> The ponderous anchor rises o'er the wave.
> High on the slippery masts the yards ascend,
> And far abroad the canvas wings extend.
>
> *   *   *   *   *   *
>
> Majestically slow before the breeze
> She moves triumphant o'er the yielding seas."

His description of a fine breeze is equally happy:

> "O'er the smooth bosom of the faithless tides,
> Propell'd by flattering gales, the vessel glides;"

and when the wind increases,

> "The lighter sails, for summer winds and seas,
> Are now dismissed, the straining masts to ease;"

and

> "The powerful sails, with steady breezes swelled,
> Swift and more swift the yielding bark impelled."

Soon a squall strikes her, and the poet's word-painting is as vivid as ever:

> "But see! In confluence borne before the blast,
> Clouds roll'd on clouds the dusky noon o'ercast:
> The blackening ocean curls, the winds arise,
> And the dark scud in swift succession flies.
> While the swoln canvas bends the masts on high,
> Low in the wave the leeward cannon lie.

The master calls, to give the ship relief,
The topsails lower, and form a single reef.
Each lofty yard with slackened cordage reels ;
Rattle the creaking blocks and ringing wheels.
Down the tall masts the topsails sink amain,
Are mann'd and reef'd, then hoisted up again."

Here follows a passage which is so true to nature
that you can almost hear the song of the sailors as
they haul the sheets block-a-block, while the vessel
heels till her gunwale kisses the crests of the waves:

"The foresail braced obliquely to the wind,
They near the prow the extended tack confined;
Then on the leeward sheet the seamen bend,
And haul the bowline to the bowsprit-end.
The mainsail, by the squall so lately rent,
In streaming pendants flying, is unbent :
With brails refixed, another soon prepared,
Ascending, spreads along beneath the yard.
To each yard-arm the head-rope they extend,
And soon their earings and their robans bend.
That task performed, they first the braces slack,
Then to the chess-tree draw the unwilling tack.
And, while the lee clew-garnet's lowered away,
Taut aft the sheet they tally, and belay."

There are in this description a vast number of what
Pope contemptuously styles "tarpaulin phrases," but
they are so skillfully and rhythmically used that they
do not mar the verse. They are noble lines, and we
enjoy them as keenly as if they had flowed from the
pen of Virgil.

I can not refrain from introducing one more quota-
tion from this poet, over whose cradle, if he had been
born in Greece, a graceful cluster of legends would
have hung, which is so wonderfully vivid that one

almost feels himself to be aboard, and begins to think seriously of his policy of life-insurance. The noble ship is staggering to a watery grave :

> " In vain the cords and axes were prepared,
> For every wave now smites the quivering yard.
> High o'er the ship they throw a dreadful shade,
> Then on her burst in terrible cascade ;
> Across the founder'd deck o'erwhelming roar,
> And foaming, swelling, bound upon the shore.
> Swift up the mounting billow now she flies,
> Her shatter'd top half buried in the skies ;
> Borne o'er a latent reef the hull impends,
> Then thundering on the marble crags descends :
> Her ponderous bulk the dire concussion feels,
> And o'er upheaving surges wounded reels—
> Again she plunges ! hark ! a second shock
> Bilges the splitting vessel on the rock—
> Down on the vale of death, with dismal cries,
> The fated victims shuddering cast their eyes
> In wild despair ; while yet another stroke
> With strong convulsion rends the solid oak :
> Ah Heaven !—behold her crashing ribs divide !
> She loosens, parts, and spreads in ruin o'er the tide."

While soliloquizing thus, the pilot came to me about noon, and, pointing to the land, said,

" That is Tracadie Harbor just opposite."

" Then we are a little more than a third of the distance to North Point. Isn't it a lovely island ! Just ahead of us there are high bluffs, while the last few miles of shore have been very level and very low. But I see no rocks—how is that ?"

" There are no rocks on the island," he replied ; " that is, none to interfere with agriculture. The soil is rich, and makes one of the best farming districts in the world."

"But with such a loose soil I should think the currents, which in a northeaster must set shoreward with great force, would wash the coast away, just as happens at Nantucket, for instance."

"It would have been washed away long ago but for the millions of clams and muscles, which are thick enough to make a kind of breakwater. Halloo, the wind gives a little—what does that mean?"

We had been going with a perfect rush, logging ten miles for the first two hours, and twelve for the last three, but suddenly, as though the wind had blown itself out, the sails began to flap, and we were as still as a "painted ship upon a painted ocean."

"John, get the bait, and Ah Boo, my Celestial beauty, get the lines, for this is one of the finest fishing coasts in the world," some one said. "See all about us a fleet of forty or fifty schooners hauling in the cod. Now for the first fish."

In five minutes our lines, all the lines on board in fact, were over.

"I have one!" and "So have I!" and "I have two!" were the successive cries from stem to stern.

That was a very neat little episode. It was dead calm for just fifteen minutes, and in that time we had brought on deck sixteen good-sized cod and haddock. Some of the cod were pale in color as though they had lived in the realms of eternal night, while others were as red as though they had been feeding on sunset.

"There she comes again," said the captain, and, sure enough, the wind filled the sails, the *Nettie* started, and in half an hour we were bounding along at the old terrific rate. What a day of smooth sailing that was!

The waves fairly glistened with sunlight, and the sea was of that deep refreshing blue which so fascinates that you can not take your eyes from it, while the air was bracing and exhilarating to the last degree. Every body was in the highest spirits. Fowler was at the wheel, and he never once let her up as the gust struck her, but kept her going at her best speed.

" This is ideal !—this is superb !" said Ruloff, as he paced the deck, striking his chest, and taking in great draughts of pure oxygen.

" Arn't you glad you were born ?" said Bertric, "and isn't every breath a separate luxury? The crotchety old fellow who said that the people who are dead and buried ought to be thankful never came to the St. Lawrence." We all responded to the sentiment, for such a day as that seldom visits our planet.

By the middle of the afternoon we were off Richmond Harbor, and before supper we had passed North Point, and laid our course for Chaleur Bay. Nothing is more interesting than to notice the peculiarities of the shore as you pass it, or call to mind the salient points in the history of the people who inhabit it. There is not a single good harbor—*i. e.*, a harbor easy of access—on the whole northern shore of Prince Edward's. Every bay is barricaded by sand-bars, and it is impossible to get in without the aid of a pilot, unless you are thoroughly acquainted. The light-houses are all good and sufficiently numerous, there being four in the ninety-five miles from west to east. It is a sorry place, however, when the wind is strong from the north, and at North Point we saw a huge three-master which had been thrown up on the sand stern first.

Sailors are not overfond of this shore, because in thick weather it is impossible to calculate one's bearing. The wind has such complete control over the tides that the water sometimes runs one way for days. No tabular account of tides in the Gulf is of any value for this reason. For instance, when a strong southerly gale is blowing, the ebb of the great river is accelerated, and the waters along the western coast of Newfoundland are piled up at the Strait of Belle Isle, and the current sets to the northward for forty-eight hours or more. When, again, the wind blows from the northeast, this accumulation of waters is driven back, and the current sets through the Gut of Canso for an equal length of time, and along the north shore of Prince Edward's with such extreme irregularity that in stormy weather a good lookout is absolutely necessary. Nothing is easier than to make a fatal mistake in this matter. The Almanac assures you that the tide is making to the southward, and in the thick fog or the cloudy darkness you lay your course accordingly; the truth may be that the southerly winds which have prevailed for a week past have piled the waters up to the northward, and that the current is still flowing at the rate of three miles an hour in that direction. And so it happens that while you are sound asleep in your berth, perfectly sure that every thing is going on well, your craft is slowly but surely drifting toward the low line of sand, which is not easily discovered in a dark night, and you are rudely awakened by the sharp grating of the keel which is the death-knell of your noble vessel.

When we were off Mirimichi, just to the westward of Cape North, and on the mainland, we read an ac-

count of the great fire which laid bare the whole country for scores of miles around in 1825. It occurred
after a long season of drought, and the dried underbrush and dead wood, together with the resinous quality of the timber, furnished material for a conflagration
which lasted for months. It filled the heavens to the
westward with black smoke, which at night glistened
with a million starry sparks, and made a spectacle
which would have been of unparalleled grandeur but
for the devastation already accomplished and the greater devastation that was threatened. On the 6th of Oc-
tober fitful blazes and flashes were seen just back of
Newcastle and Douglastown, while the woods all along
the banks of the Bartibogue were filled with the crackling and falling timber. The whole firmament seemed
wrapped in a vengeful pall of vapor. Huge masses of
black cloud cut through by flashes of fire, as though
riven by lightning, settled down on the whole region,
while the dull thunder of the fire-fiend's progress shook
the hearts of the people all along the coast. This
smoke so thoroughly pervaded the atmosphere that it
produced upon the inhabitants an unaccountable lassi-
tude and stupefaction. Showers of flaming brands fell
on the little towns, which were as rapidly consumed
as so much tinder. A hurricane, the necessary consequence of so much heat, bore the huge clouds aloft,
until they looked like the black minarets of some demon's temple, while the crash of falling timber and the
sullen roar of the fire sent dismay into a thousand
hearts. The river was lashed to fury by the wind, and
threw its boiling spray far up the shore. It resembled
in its windings and its agonies an immense serpent in

its death agony, writhing, tossing, tumbling, and moaning in its fury. You can form some dim conception of the scene if you will imagine a conflagration extending more than one hundred miles over the country, and covering an area of nearly six thousand square miles of township and forest. In the river were something like one hundred and fifty vessels, some of which were burned to the water's edge, while others, burning and drifting down on their neighbors, set fire to their rigging and sails. More than five hundred human beings were consumed, and thousands of wild beasts, which afterward filled the air with pestilent contagion.

After reciting all these scenes to each other, we set our watches for the night and went to bed.

CHAPTER XI.

CHALEUR AND PERCÈ.

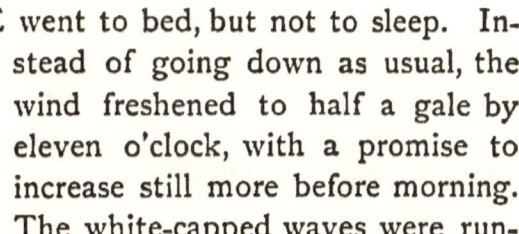 E went to bed, but not to sleep. In-
stead of going down as usual, the
wind freshened to half a gale by
eleven o'clock, with a promise to
increase still more before morning.
The white-capped waves were run-
ning high, and every few minutes we took a mountain
of water on board which rushed like an avenging flood
over the deck. I tried in vain to get into a doze, but
though I wooed sleep in the most persistent manner,
she was very coy, and refused to come near me. At
one time I would lie flat on my back, when the vessel
rolled and pitched in such unexpected directions that I
was most unceremoniously tumbled from one side of
the berth to the other. Then I curled my knees up
and braced them against the side, determined not to
yield, but in a moment I was bounced out of position,
and bumped against the edge of the berth with such
force that I determined to surrender unconditionally,
and so got up and dressed. But dressing under such
circumstances is no light task. I sat down on a chair
to put my stockings on, and the next moment found
myself sprawling on the floor, my legs in air, and my

head suffering from contact with the corner of my trunk. Now I leaned up against the door in the hope of successfully performing that series of gymnastics through which one goes when he tries to get into his pantaloons, but a sudden lurch threw me, when the work was half completed, against the berth, and managed to snarl up legs, pants, and arms in an inextricable tangle. After a while, however, I succeeded in getting into my clothes, and finding my way on deck. The heavens were very dark, and the water was dashing about the bows in such a furious manner that all I could see forward of the foremast was an avalanche of foam. All around us, as far as eye could reach, the sea was a roaring, tumbling mass of white-caps.

A night on the water out of sight of land is a very pleasant experience. One is constantly under the illusion that he sees lights, that he hears the booming of guns, or the solemn toll of the fog-bell. To one not yet accustomed to the ocean this is exceedingly painful. He looks away to the starboard, or over on the port hand, and is morally certain that not far off he detects a light or hears a noise, and has the feeling that the pilot has mistaken his course, and that the vessel is going directly on shore. Then every thing is magnified at night: the waves seem higher, the wind blows more fiercely, the ship heels over more, the rigging is straining, and pretty nearly every thing is coming to pieces.

The captain seemed very cheery, however, and that reassured me completely.

" Isn't the old girl just trotting along !" he said, as he took a seat by my side.

"Yes; but don't you think it a wild sort of night?"
I suggested.

"Wild? Oh, no," he replied; "one could not ask
for a better time than this. The top-hamper is all
snugly stowed, we have a free wind, and are jogging on
at the rate of twelve knots by the log. What can any
man want more?"

I brought the wolf-robe and a pillow on deck, and
never enjoyed any thing so much in my life. The
Nettie would struggle up a huge wave until she turned
the summit, and then rush down the other side as
though she were bound to bury herself under the next
boulder. Indeed, it has always seemed to me a miracle that a vessel should rise just at the right moment.
Why she does not contrive to sink when once she begins is a mystery. But when she has thrust her jib-
boom into the wave ahead of her, and it is on the very
point of coming aboard, and is curling and cresting for
that purpose, hesitating before taking the final leap,
the bows begin to lift, the stern settles down, and the
danger is over. How many times I have sat at the
cat-head and watched a huge seventh or tenth wave as
it came on in its magnificence, and felt certain that its
crystal walls would break at the bows, and that we
should be flooded by a deck-load of salt water. The
vessel has risen to the top of the wave, and then com-
menced that descent which produces such a peculiar
and unpleasant feeling in the abdominal regions of sen-
sitive natures. She plunges headlong into the boiling
mass entirely reckless of consequences, and, before you
have recovered from the shiver that runs through you,
she groans as she dashes the water away, and slowly,

oh, so slowly at first that your heart sinks within you, rises, with only a few bucketfuls of the briny splash on deck.

With the same kind of wonder I have watched a horse manipulate, as it were, his feet. It has always seemed a miracle that his hind-feet never tread on his fore-feet, for the most natural thing in the world would be for his hind-quarters to run over the fore-quarters. The front-foot clings to the pavement until the hind-foot comes within half an inch of it, when, just in the nick of time, it is got out of the way, only to be put in the same dangerous position the next moment. I have looked at this spectacle, which has a kind of fascination, until I have grown so nervous that I had to hold on to the seat, momentarily expecting the creature to fairly run over himself, or roll himself up in a ball.

At about two o'clock the next morning Ruloff showed his head above the companion-way with a—

"Well, captain, what are you doing?"

"Doing nothing but going ahead, and that at a spanking pace, too."

"I wish you wouldn't make so much fuss about it, though," continued Ruloff; "not a wink of sleep have I had yet. That berth of mine is as uneasy as a chestnut in the fire. I have been knocked about until I feel like an enormous bruise."

"Old Boreas is doing his best to-night," cried Stigand, as he emerged soon after. And at that, as though in proof of his assertion, the wind quietly lifted his hat from his head, carried it half way up the mainsail, and then bore it triumphantly away.

I

"Well, that's a pretty trick to play a fellow who hasn't closed his eyes all night," he continued; and then did what every man does who loses his hat under similar circumstances—that is, suddenly put both hands on his head, with the idea that an imaginary hat is still there, or under the delusion that his hair will soon follow his hat. Every body slaps his head when he loses his hat. It may be that the wind communicates the information to the muscles of the arm at the instant the hat begins to rise, and the arm and hand are a little sluggish in their movements, or it may be for some other metaphysical reason which I am unable to give; but I never yet saw a man lose his hat without immediately clutching his hair.

Perhaps it would be no more than fair to give another reason for the general appearance of the gentlemen on deck that night. I have referred to the costly purchase of a fox in a previous chapter. Allow me now to recall an episode in which he was one of the chief actors. While the novelty of his presence lasted he was allowed to do pretty much as he pleased, and his antics were of the most grotesque kind. He was not a particle afraid of the dog, who in lumbering fashion chased him over the deck, when at length, tired of the little game, Reynard would make a short turn, run back on his track, and get into a snug hiding-place, while the dog, in the vain attempt to turn suddenly, tripped over a coil of rope, and rolled over and over. The little dog—we had two on board—which was one of the tiniest of black-and-tans, by no means so large as the fox, would once in a while resent the continued teasing of Reynard, who delighted to walk over him or lie down on him when he felt disposed to take a nap, and with a growl which displayed his white teeth to perfection would set on him. At such times the fox, whose offensive weapons did not lie in his jaws, would suddenly wheel round and present the other end of himself to the dog, who fastened his teeth into the fur, and generally came out of the conflict with such a mouthful of hair that for the next half-hour he was perfectly miserable.

On this particular night the fox got loose, and roamed at his own sweet will. With his long chain attached to his neck, he came rattling down the cabin steps, which were covered with brass, ran around among the table and chair legs and into the kitchen, with such resounding and distracting noise that sleep became an impossibility. Bertric got up, *en déshabillé*, and chased him. But in the dark it was no easy task to catch the fellow. What with the rolling and pitching of the vessel, added to the miraculous gyrations of the fox, it is not to be wondered at if a few plain English words expressed the utter disgust of Bertric at being compelled to engage in a fox-chase at midnight when it was difficult to keep one's feet under the most propitious circumstances.

"There, you rascal! I've got you!" he cried at length, as he grasped the fur on the back of Mr. Fox. "You hideous wretch! why did we ever pay two dollars and a half for you?" Then he continued in a delightful monologue: "And why wern't you content with your native woods, instead of spoiling the tempers of Christian folk? Ugh! how cold it is!"

The poor fellow shivered as he carried the animal

on deck, struggling all the while to get loose, and chained him, as he thought, securely to his barrel.

He had, however, no sooner returned to his berth than the same rattling was heard, and with a groan of despair Bertric turned over in his berth, muttering,

"Well, some one else must try his hand at that thing this time. I'm actually shivering with cold, and won't get up again for all the foxes that ever stole chickens."

A general chuckle was heard, which showed that the gentlemen were all awake, and had enjoyed the episode.

Pretty soon the fox jumped through one of the deadlights, and landed, chain and all, on the cabin floor, with a noise which compelled a dismal "Oh dear!" to come from behind every curtain. Reynard leaped into one of the berths with the expectation of snuggling down for the night, when the occupant defeated his good intentions by giving him a push which sent him into the middle of the cabin. This experiment was tried on every sleeper, until at last Stigand, in sheer desperation, got up, saying, "I'm going to throw that fellow overboard;" and, grabbing him in a way that indicated earnestness of character, carried him back to his barrel, where he was made so fast that the knot was untied with great difficulty the next day.

What a magnificent sunrise we had the next morning! I saw it, not because I wanted to, but because I had to. I would have greatly preferred to be quietly asleep, and to have taken the grandeur of the occasion on the word of another, but nevertheless it was a sight not to be forgotten. The dull, gray clouds had settled in the eastern horizon in huge masses, while above long stretches of dark vapor lay athwart the sky. A faint tint of red suffused them all at first, and then it deepened, until the whole heavens in that direction seemed to fairly blaze with rich glory. Then the upper disk of the sun was seen just above the horizon, and soon after the full round orb, of an orange color, which brightened until the eye could no longer look upon it, and day was fairly upon us.

"Land on the port bow!" cried John.

It was Miscou Island, at the southern entrance to Chaleur Bay—at least so the pilot affirmed.

"Impossible!" we all cried at once. "We can not have come so far in so short a time."

"Let her off a point," said the captain to the man at the wheel. "Come aft, now, and ease the sheets. There, that will do; now let her travel."

And we did travel. The yacht felt the slackening of the sheets, and we fairly whizzed through the water.

"We shall sight Bonaventura in an hour," prophesied Edwards, "and then you will see ducks, if you never saw them before."

What a grand sheet of water Chaleur Bay is, to be sure. It is the finest and largest harbor in the Gulf of St. Lawrence. It is about twenty-five miles wide at its mouth, and runs inland to the mouth of the Restigouche nearly seventy-five miles. About twenty-two miles to the eastward of Miscou is a huge sand-bank with from twenty to thirty fathoms of water, and there at almost any season are to be seen scores of schooners fishing for cod.

Sure enough, in an hour the lookout cried, "Land right ahead!" and we were within ten miles of Bonaventura. It is a picturesque spot, with perpendicular cliffs of red sandstone two hundred and fifty feet high to the seaward, and falling off at the westerly end to a pebbly beach.

In these rocky cliffs thousands of gannets and tens of thousands of medrakes and cormorants build their houses. When we were just opposite we fired our guns, and there arose from the great fissures in the cliff flocks of birds so numerous that we were fairly startled.

"Now for sport!" cried Fletch. "We'll run into Percè, and have such a day's shooting as those birds have never heard tell of."

"Oh, you can shoot till you are tired, and there will be plenty of game left for the next comer," said Edwards, quietly.

The *Nettie* was put on the other tack—not an easy thing to accomplish in such a heavy sea—during which few minutes we were tossed so furiously that it seemed as if every line in the vessel would snap, and then we bounded along at a great rate for the little, but, except in a southwest wind, dangerous harbor of Percè.

Percè is one of the neatest villages I ever visited. Its inhabitants are French, and they retain with undaunted persistency the simplicity which has always been attributed to the Acadians. The few streets of the village are smooth and well taken care of. The houses are all comfortable, and have a decided air of thrift about them. Just in the rear of the village rises Mount Percè, or Table Roulante, as it is sometimes called, to the unusual height of 1230 feet above the sea-level, and visible from a distance of forty miles.

It is well wooded, but has a fair forest-road leading to the summit, from which the scenery is too exquisite to be described. The fishermen, who compose the inhabitants of the village, set their nets regularly at sunrise, and gather in their spoils at sundown. A hundred boats are shoved off from the beach every day, while the air is filled with the rollicking songs of the toilers. They are a happy, honest folk, and the manufactories where the fish are cured are models of neatness and business thrift. Nowhere on the coast is such another spot to be found.

The next morning Fletch and I went out of town to a little stream just back of Table Roulante, and enjoyed a few hours of fine trout-fishing. The game was not large, but numerous. We creeled several dozen, but our pleasure was somewhat lessened by the army of mosquitoes and black flies which attacked every exposed part of our persons. To this pest the midge joined forces, and altogether we had many more bites than fish. However, the drive into the country and along the beautiful beach just west of the village repaid us for our temporary unhappiness, and we returned to the yacht, with our speckled treasures and mottled faces, with an appetite which no city life has any conception of. And here let me observe that one of the charms of yachting is the appetite it develops, and the general physical condition it induces. One is necessarily in the open air all the time. By day, though lounging about on deck, he is conscious of the upbuilding that is going on in his system, and by night he sleeps with the sky-light and the dead-lights open, which makes the boat the equivalent of a tent in the woods. The wind whistles through, and he wakes in the morning as fresh as a daisy, and with a perfect willingness to engage in any undertaking, however arduous. It is worth something to have one's animal spirits at high-water mark; and it is a good sign when one tumbles out of his berth, not lazily and languidly, as though he had just been through an ordeal and scarcely survived it, but with a leap and a jump, as though sleep had done its work in getting him into good fighting condition.

"Cup coffee, sir?" said Ah Boo every morning at about six. That was his only matutinal greeting; and then, knowing what the answer would be, he hurried to the kitchen with a low chuckle to get the delicious compound.

"Coffee, steward? Yes, and any thing else you can find on board in the way of eatables," was the usual answer sent after his retreating form.

At sea one's digestive apparatus gets into admirable working order, and it is absolutely necessary to keep a good lookout for the commissary department.

"Now then," said Ruloff, after dinner had been disposed of, "let's be off to Arch Rock."

I have left this magnificent piece of nature to the present moment that I might bring it out in strong relief. It is one of the curiosities of the continent, and well repays a visit from any distance. It is an abrupt, precipitous rock, that rises perpendicularly from the water to the height of nearly three hundred feet, and in its contour is not unlike a huge vessel. We approached its bows, the western end, and it seemed to us very like the *Great Eastern,* which had come to anchor on this northern coast. At the Percè end it is sharp like the bows of a vessel, while at the other end it rounds like its stern. It is about fifteen hundred feet long, and has two natural arches, through which boats can float at high tide, and one of which is plainly visible many miles at sea.

When one lands at its base he is compelled, as it were, to look twice before his vision reaches the top ; that is, he looks at a point that is as high as he has before conceived the rock to be, and finds that it is only half-way up. Then, after resting his eyes for a moment, he looks far up into the distance, and sees there overhanging edges of rough, rugged rock, which seem as if they were about to fall and crush him. We sat or lay down on the beach, scarcely speaking to each other for a full half-hour, perfectly satisfied with simply gazing at the monster.

Then Fletch was called back from his reverie by a huge yellowish plover strutting along the shore. Poor plover! his time had come to be metamorphosed into one of the ingredients of a pie, and he submitted to his fate without a murmur. Our journey round the base of the rock was a constant surprise. Here, for instance, was a pebbly beach in the shape of a horse-shoe, and about fifty feet long, while immediately behind it was a cavern in the rock, hollowed out by the waves of a thousand years, the sides of which were as smooth as polished marble. There, just beyond, was the first arch, about ten feet high, and twelve or fifteen feet wide. The tide ebbed and flowed through it, and it looked more like the well-calculated handiwork of man than the result of natural forces. And there

I 2

again, farther on, was the large arch, about twenty feet high, and perhaps twenty-five broad, which we had seen when six or eight miles away, and which gives the rock its name.

We scrambled through it, and got a grand view of the rock from the other side; then determined to come down from the poetical to the practical by trying our guns on the various kinds of birds which filled the air. Imagination alone can compute the numbers of gulls and cormorants which inhabit this romantic spot, for no human arithmetic can approximate to the sum total. We paddled off almost twenty rods from the rock, and looking up saw every ledge that jutted out from this entire surface literally packed with birds. When they flew, they flew in enormous crowds, and their choral screeches could be heard at a fabulous distance. We were told that on the top of the rock are tens of thousands of eggs; that in former times an adventurer would once in a while scale the dizzy height for purposes of curiosity or gain, but that the feat was of such a dangerous nature that a law had been recently passed prohibiting it under severe penalty. But besides the danger of climbing these unruly crags, some of which are unpleasantly loose, and give under one's weight, is to be taken into account the fierce onslaughts of the birds. It is as much as a man's life is worth to invade the possessions of the gulls. It may seem very like a sailor's yarn to say that these creatures in immense numbers are a formidable enemy, but such nevertheless is the truth. They can not be frightened by the discharge of a gun, for they are exceedingly loyal in their parental love, nor can they be beaten off with clubs. They swoop down on one with a kind of war-whoop, and with their sharp bills make sad havoc with one's clothes and flesh, and have a particular fancy for one's eyes. At any rate, the inhabitants of the village, though covetous of gulls' eggs, have no inclination to risk themselves on the top of Arch Rock.

After a few discharges of our guns, a division of the grand army took its flight, and in dizzy circles cut the air above our heads. We managed, after patiently waiting for them to return from their lofty height, to drop a few of the medrakes, whose wings seemed to be in demand, and one or two of the immense gray gulls, which have bodies no larger than a full-grown chicken, but wings large enough to carry a good-sized boy well up toward the moon. The cormorants are also huge birds, with coarse, dissonant voices, and wings as dark as night. They look clumsy as geese in the distance, with their long necks stretched out, but they manage to keep out of range in their rapid flight. All over the water were scattered sea-pigeons, which can be had in any numbers. They are too fishy to satisfy an ordinary palate, though they do very well as a side dish.

The next morning it was blowing heavily, and, as the wind threatened a change, we determined to get away as soon as possible. So our anchor was weighed, and we started across Mal Bay for the Bay of Gaspe.

Gaspe Bay is very small in comparison with Chaleur Bay, but in many respects it is not less important or remarkable. At its entrance, and on the northeast side, is Cape Gaspe, a headland of limestone, the terminus of a magnificent range of cliffs, which rise nearly seven hundred feet above the sea-level, and in many places are almost perpendicular. On the south side the shore is also very bold, and several good-sized streams pour over the bluffs in a white sheet of snowy foam, adding greatly to the fascinations of a very charming landscape. As you enter the bay the scene is of the most ravishing description. The shore to the right is quite thickly settled by fishermen, whose little cottages, with the background of forest and foreground of water, are romantic to the last degree. On the left, just within the bay, and beyond Red Head, is the town of Douglas, where vessels can find a good harbor with still water. And away off in the distance, right before you, rise the mountains, upon whose tops the clouds seem to settle, as though they took pride in making the picture perfect.

But the most curious and valuable peculiarity of Gaspe is what is called the Basin. This is a sheet of water at the northwestern end of the bay, on which the town of Gaspe is situated, so entirely landlocked that it is as quiet as a mill-pond, even in the roughest weather. No matter how or which way the wind blows, not the faintest perceptible undulation, not even the dimmest and most indistinct echo of a swell, ever intrudes. It is an ideal anchorage, large enough to accommodate a fleet, and with water enough to float the largest of them all.

Having come to anchor here, with the expectation of spending about a week on the salmon rivers and in the woods, we filled up our ice-chest and water-tanks, and made arrangements to have the commissary well taken care of. This was the farthest point north we in-

tended to make. It would have been delightful to have
run over to Anticosti, but thirty miles away, or across
to the Mingan Islands and the Labrador coast, about
fifty more, but one's appetite is never satisfied, and so
we left these things for another year. There is something wonderful about ocean traveling. You may
go as far as you please, but you always want to see
the next place. You are never satisfied, but forever
dreaming of new pleasures and new discoveries for
the morrow. Our time was limited, however, and we
were compelled to restrain at once our curiosity and
our love of adventure.

There are only about one or two hundred inhabitants
in Gaspe, part of which, those on the northerly side of
the Basin, are English and Scotch, while the rest, those
on the southerly side, are French. There is one church
in the village, the Episcopal, finely situated on the
side of a hill, overlooking the northern arm, but with
such interior accommodations that the patience of the
saintly is severely tried, while the temper of the pro-
fane is lost entirely. We worshiped with the little
congregation one afternoon, and marveled that it was
possible to crowd so much discomfort into so small a
space. Why is it, I wonder, that you are allowed, at
home, to sit in a chair with such an incline to its back
that you are rested, while in some churches to sit
down is torture, and to stand up is impossible ? If I
had a boy whom I wanted to bring up in such fashion
that he would never cross the threshold of a church
after his twenty-first birthday, I would send him to some
village church like that at Gaspe, or like most of the
churches along the coast, where he could neither lean

back nor yet sit up straight, but must needs lean forward just enough to be wretched, and endure the torment of having the ornamental rim on the top of the pew cut across his back. If he did not eschew all forms of religion after that, it would be because his parentage was too much for him.

We paid a visit the next day to the customs officers, who were very kind and considerate to us as owners of a vessel from foreign parts, and also to the gentlemanly American consul, who gave us a refreshing peep into New York and Boston papers.

For a day or two we simply rested, only diverting ourselves by a ride of a few miles into the country, reading and writing letters, fishing from the deck of the yacht, or catching a few smelt nearer shore. The Indians, who have an insignificant settlement a few miles back of the town, brought us fresh strawberries every morning, and a farmer supplied us with rich cream. In point of comfort, if not of luxury, therefore, our position was one not exactly to be despised.

CHAPTER XII.

INDIAN CANOES.

OME up, gentlemen!" cried Stigand, the next morning after breakfast; "here are some Indians coming aboard."

"What!" said Bertric, "real, live Indians? Oh, my scalp!"

"They are only Mic-Macs," said Ruloff; "a very gentle and harmless race. You can keep the capillaries on your crown until you lose them by natural process."

"Yes, but isn't the knife of a Mic-Mac as sharp as that of a Choctaw?" responded Bertric; "and does it make any difference by whom you lose your scalp, if only you lose it? I don't like the noble red man. The roots of my hair begin to tingle at the very thought of him."

"You needn't be afraid of these fellows; they are as tame as sheep, and only want to sell wild strawberries, and go fishing with you."

So we all rushed up to see the Micks, as some one called them. They were a couple of stalwart fellows, tawny as tanned leather, with long black hair streaming down on their shoulders. They wore no scalps at their belt, neither did they brandish a tomahawk.

"Go fishing, sir?" said one of them to me.

"What kind of fish do you get, John?"

"Trout—white trout, so long," making a motion with his hands, which left me somewhat in doubt whether he meant to measure off a foot or a yard. "Brook trout too — O, very much big; and ducks plenty."

"Where do you go to get them?"

"Up Dartmouth. Only five miles. Back by night."

"How do you get there?"

"In canoe. Dad has one—I have one."

"Are those things easy to get into?" asked Ruloff.

"Yes," broke in Bertric, "and a good deal easier to get out of, I should judge."

They were very pretty canoes, and altogether the excursion was a tempting one. Two kinds of trout, a long talk with real Indians, a ride in a canoe, and perhaps a few wood-ducks would make a very agreeable day's sport; so we agreed to start the next morning at eight.

There is no prettier sailing than in a birch. After you once get used to it, and can balance yourself, the motion is rhythmic and delightful. It does not cut through the water as does an ordinary boat—with a constant splash at the bows—but seems to glide over the surface, as though it scarcely deigned to touch it. Light as an egg-shell, the sturdy strength of the guide drives it along at an inconceivable pace.

When I was younger, and used to frequent the wilds of Maine, I became greatly enamored of this mode of traveling. I distinctly remember my first experience, and laugh even now when I recall the incident which left me a "moist, unpleasant body." My guide—I had engaged him the day before—came trudging along the road with the birch on his shoulder. He was a man of rare beauty. Full six feet high, with a chest which a *basso profondo* would have envied, he handled the canoe as easily as you or I would a gun. When we reached the river bank, he gave it a light and graceful toss, and it fell like a huge snow-flake in the stream about seven feet from shore. Then, thrusting one end of his long paddle into the bottom of the river, and bearing a part of his weight on the other, he gave a spring and landed in the canoe, which seemed to be as steady under him as a man-of-war.

The feat was performed with such apparent ease that the real difficulty of achieving it was hidden from my sight. I was tempted by an evil spirit to make the experiment myself.

" Come out, Harry, and see me do that." In an instant he was by my side, handing me the paddle, but with just the shadow of an incredulous look on his face, which made me more determined than ever to astonish him by my agility and skill. So, imitating my leader, I stuck the blade of my paddle into the bottom, and, holding firmly to the other end, sprang. Somehow I think the knack of the thing is more in the way in which you strike than in the way in which you jump. I accomplished the feat to perfection until that critical and decisive moment when my feet touched the bottom of the canoe, but at that point something evidently went wrong. Either I had jumped too far or not far enough, but in less time than it requires to put these words on paper the canoe like a thing of life slipped from under my feet, and bounded off into the middle of the river, while I found myself taking a lesson in the art of swimming rather than in that of canoeing. Harry waded in and recovered his birch, after which I made the same experiment a full dozen times, tumbling into the river with an ominous splash at nearly every attempt, but at last doing it well enough to insure dry clothes on another occasion.

I remember those days so well that I would fain linger over them for a while. We poled up to Gordon Falls, with the exception of a short portage, the next day, and were rewarded by a fine catch of trout. It was a region difficult of access, and very little fished. The river was about a hundred feet wide, with overhanging woods on either bank. At night we camped in the most primitive fashion. Cutting two uprights, about seven feet long, with a cross-piece to fit the crotches on the upper end, we had the framework of the house. Branches of trees thatched our cottage completely, while our mattresses were made of fragrant hemlock boughs. He who has never slept on a hemlock bed has something yet to live for. Then we cut a huge pile of wood, whose crackling and cheerful blaze would keep us company all night, and were happy. We lived, too, like princes. Hard bread with fried pork will make a meal which hungry gods might relish; and a pound trout, freshly caught, with a slice of pork laid carefully between his ribs, rolled up in the largest leaves that can be found, then laid to rest on a hot flat stone until it is exactly cooked, makes a dish which no man in his senses and with a normal appetite would refuse.

But the exciting part of that experience was in running the rapids. When traveling in quick water, and over somewhat uneven surfaces, it is very difficult to keep the canoe perfectly balanced, for the slightest preponderance of weight on the one side or the other is apt to result in a wetting, if nothing more.

We shoved off from our camping-ground into the smooth water of an eddy. The rapids were nearly a quarter of a mile long, with here and there sharp, quick turns to the right and left. I took my position in the stern, sitting in the bottom of the canoe, while Harry stood at the stem, pole in hand.

"Now, sir, keep steady, and we'll take the current."

"Yes, that I will; not a muscle shall be moved, and I'll stop winking if you say so."

In a moment the birch felt the quick water, and began to move down stream, slowly at first, but pretty soon as rapidly as I care to travel in that kind of conveyance. We sped along with increasing velocity as we approached the rapids, while the trees on the banks seemed to be moving away from us. At one moment, Harry, by a movement which seemed as quick as the thought that prompted it, drove his long pole into the pebbly bottom, and gave the light canoe a shove which sent her into the roaring, boiling waters, and at another he took advantage of an eddy, and laid his course in smooth water for the next few rods. Once he saw a smooth mossy stone, just ahead, and only about three inches under the surface; and with a skill and energy which I envied at the time, and have continued to envy ever since, he planted the end of his pole against a boulder, and pushed the birch bodily away. At another time, however, he was nearly caught. We were rushing at a headlong speed between two masses of rock where the water seemed to be quite deep, when for a single breath the bottom of the canoe stranded, or threatened to strand, on a piece of sunken, slippery, water-logged timber. Thirty seconds' stay in such a position and the canoe would have been hogged, as the sailors say when a vessel's bottom is strained out of shape, but Harry, who was heavier than I, ran his pole into the sand, and actually hung to it, only touching the birch with his feet to steady it, until the danger was passed.

"Harry, do you propose to go over the fall?" I said, thinking that I had had pretty nearly enough of such exciting sport.

"Yes, sir, there's no help for it now," he replied. "If we try to land we shall be carried against that rock, and then you'll have to swim ashore."

The fall was just ahead, and I confess that at the time I preferred to witness the scene rather than be a part of it. It was no very formidable fall, being only about five feet high, with plenty of water, still I was not anxious to go over it.

"Now, sir, steady as you can, and don't move, whatever happens."

With that he laid the pole on the thwarts, and took to the paddle. He got steerage way on, even in that quick water, by a few vigorous strokes, and the moment of catastrophe or success approached. I can only remember that I saw him projected over the edge of the fall a few feet, while I and my end of the canoe

seemed to be sinking down into the caldron of seeth-
ing waters, and the next moment I heard a splash,
which threw the spray all over me, as we struck the
surface below.

"All right, sir," said Harry.

"That was well done, old fellow," I responded;
"and you shall have a pound of tobacco for that
feat."

"Thank you, sir. I was only afraid you would move,
and then—"

"Well, what then, Harry?"

"I should have gone overboard after you, that is
all."

And I believe he would have done it.

Now for Gaspe once more. The next morning, at
the time appointed, our red men made their appearance. They were not got up in the picturesque style of
the Indians of our imagination, nor did they have the
euphonious names in which we take so much delight.

"I certainly hoped one might be called at least
Eagle Eye," said Bertric, as he put his traps into the
birch. "How delightful it would be to go to the famous hunting-grounds with Leaping Panther, for instance."

"Well, what are their names?" asked Algar.

"This one is called John Bass, and that old fellow
in the other canoe rejoices in the simple title of Dad,"
answered Bertric.

Neither of our guides had eagle pinions in his hair,
which had not seen a comb for I know not how long.
Their heads were not ornamented with particolored

feathers, but covered with old felt hats; and their feet, so far from having on them brilliant moccasins, worked by the fair hands of Indian maidens, were encased in number eleven boots, made by machinery. The only scalps they wore were their own, and they grew eloquent only once, when they were characterizing a certain man who had swindled them out of two dollars and a half.

"Rods all in?"

"Aye, aye."

"Do we want guns, John Bass?"

"Mebbe yes, mebbe no."

"Then let us take the chances on that 'mebbe yes,'" was suggested, and we safely stowed away a rifle and a shot-gun.

"Any deer, John?"

"Praps."

"Now then, boys, tumble in, and we'll be off."

We went off in high spirits, two of us in each canoe, sitting on a matting on the bottom, and back to back. It was a lovely day, and we sang our way by the nearest point, when the scene that opened before us was beyond description, and so grand and ravishing that we forgot to laugh or joke. For miles the river, in some places more than a mile wide, stretched its lazy length along the land, while high hills rose on either side, and far beyond the mountains with their interminable forests. The sun poured his wealth of glory on the waters, until the rippling waves shone like burnished steel. The clouds assumed all sorts of fantastic shapes, which one could never tire of watching, while the air was so full of oxygen that each fresh draught of its delicious

coolness made us feel more grateful for mere existence.

We fished along the banks, hoping to catch a white
trout or two, but none took heed of our flies. At last
we turned a bend of the river, about six miles from the
starting-point, and ran across a raft of timbers which
completely blocked our passage. At first we thought
our day's sport would end in disappointment and disgust, but the pluck of the guides was equal to the
emergency. By dint of thrusting logs aside and lifting the canoes over them, we managed to work our
way along to the unobstructed stream beyond. Then
we cast our flies again, but still to no purpose. Neither
the fiery red nor the white moth seemed to have any
effect. At last I landed, determined to find my way
alone through the woods and along the bank for a
time, while the rest sat in the canoes thinking hard
thoughts. There is something grand in the primeval
forest, and the communion with nature is so complete
at such times that one is well repaid for every effort
made to reach this sublime stillness. I sat for a little
behind a quantity of brushwood meditating on the
scene, when I heard a rustle of wings just beyond.
Peeping through the parted branches I saw four ducks
gossiping with each other not ten rods off. They
were perfect beauties—clumsy enough when on the
land, but graceful as possible on the water. They were
not aware of the danger that impended, and went on
in their play, just as though double-barreled breech-
loaders had not been invented. They would swim
apart for a while intent on the food which attracted
their attention, and anon came close together and

rubbed their bills against one another, uttering little sharp sounds, which were not as musical to my ears as they doubtless were to their own.

It seemed too bad to make havoc among them, but the hunter's instinct was too strong in me to be checked long; so, without the crackling of a single twig, I crept within sight of the canoes, when I waved my handkerchief at Fletch, who immediately took the cue and landed with his Scott.

"Hush, boy, or they will hear you. Four ducks are sitting on the stream just beyond that clump of bushes. Creep up as gently as though you were treading on velvet, and we'll have a good dinner."

I do like to see a good hunter crawl up to his game. He takes no step without first looking to see where to plant his foot. The slightest noise and his chances are lost. Fletch knew his business by heart, and in a moment we were both looking at the beauties through the bushes.

"Wait till they put their heads together, Fletch, which they are sure to do in a minute or two, and then let them have one barrel. After that, if one escapes, take him on the wing."

Oh, that breathless, anxious moment, when the hunter is taking sight, and before he presses his finger on the fatal trigger. I can never get over the impression that it is the one important moment of a man's life. Success is happiness, and defeat is untold misery, when the smoke clears away, and you look over the field.

Fletch is a careful boy, and a good shot. Just at the instant when the ducks were gathered into a heap, possibly to listen to some bit of fresh gossip, I heard a report. Immediately after, another. Rushing to the bank, I saw two ducks lying very still on the water, while the third had just dropped with a delightful splash about five rods off.

"Three out of four is good shooting," I said with a shout. "They are noble fellows, and shot through the head. Won't we have a feast to-morrow, though."

He was chagrined that he had lost the fourth bird; but who ever saw a hunter perfectly satisfied?

"No fish here, John Bass," I said to the guide. "We haven't had a single bite yet, and I don't believe you ever saw a trout in this stream."

"Oh, in winter plenty trout, big fellows; big as that," and he put his hand on his paddle to indicate a measurement which might have suited a shark, but which never applied to a trout.

"Praps up there," he continued, pointing to a little side stream on the left.

"We'll go there, then; it's better to have a 'praps' than a certainty the other way."

We had no sooner struck into this stream than the indications took a favorable turn. I chanced to cast my fly on a pool when a good-sized trout rose to it, and hooked himself. From that moment our listlessness was gone. Bertric saw ahead of us what he thought to be a succession of deep pools, and as we could not get to them without wading, we plunged into the water up to our waists.

"Just look there, fellows. Did you ever see any thing like it? why, it's a perfect aquarium."

K

It was a sight to stir the blood in the heart of the most placid fisherman. There were three successive pools, apparently about nine or ten feet deep, overhung completely by branches which rendered it difficult to cast a fly, and in each one there were from six to a dozen trout, some weighing about three quarters of a pound, and a few running close up to two pounds.

First Stigand dropped a red hackle just over their noses as lightly as a feather, when two fish rose to it, and in the *mêlée* neither was hooked. Then Bertric threw his fly up stream, and let it float down within reach. Immediately a trout worth having was fast. He was too big to haul directly in, but after being played for two or three minutes he quietly succumbed to fate, and was captured.

We stayed by those pools for an hour and a half. When the fish became wary we changed our flies, and still continued the deceit. Twice we rested the pools for ten minutes, and ended the day's sport by bringing to creel as handsome a mess of trout as I have ever seen caught.

By five o'clock, however, we gave up, and turned our faces homeward. The air was getting chilly, and we were thoroughly soaked.

No one who has not experienced it can imagine the beauty of afternoon colors among the mountains and on the waters. A kind of sombre gray pervades every thing, and one naturally settles himself down to reverie. We were all the more inclined to do this, since we were both tired and hungry. As I sat in the canoe, Fletch asked the guide some questions about deer, and for an hour, or until we had nearly reached the yacht, I went off into dreamland, reviving the scenes of years agone, when I killed my first deer in the White Mountains. That morning two dogs had been taken into the woods before daybreak, and by seven we heard their distant bay. They were on a deer's track evidently, and chasing him to the water. My friend and I had taken our positions on the grassy bank of the Ammonoosuc, just opposite the roadway of the game. I had dropped into a half-doze when I heard the bushes part on the other bank, and saw a fine fat buck rush into the water to cool himself. He had fallen on his knees apparently, for nothing but his head was visible. I sat watching him, when my friend said, somewhat rudely, " Why in the world don't you shoot, man ?"

The truth was, I had forgotten all about shooting, and was engaged in admiring his graceful outlines and motions.

It was the first deer I had ever seen in the woods, and I was no exception to the general rule that every body misses his first shot at such large game. I ran my eye along the barrel of the gun and fired. The bullet did not probably go within a rod of him. At any rate, he stood up amazed for a moment, and then started for cover with a series of bounds which were so rhythmic that I have thought since it was a cruelty to shoot him. But I was on my mettle, having so disgraced myself the minute before, and this time took careful aim, and blew the top of his head off. He dropped into the rapid current, when I rushed in and dragged him ashore.

" Halloo !   There's the *Nettie*," and in ten minutes
we were aboard.

" Ah Boo, is supper ready ?"

" All ready, sir."

" So are we."

CHAPTER XIII.

ENOUGH, AND HOME.

"Such is the patriot's boast, where'er we roam,
His first, best country ever is at home."
GOLDSMITH.

UR stay in Gaspe was very delightful, but we had been so long from home that we were not sorry to turn the bows of the *Nettie* in that direction. I hoped, as I have already said, to be able to land on the romantic and, in many respects, remarkable island of Anticosti, but time, the inexorable, would not allow. I have dreams of some day cruising along the whole coast of Labrador, east of the Mingan Islands, and making a bold push through the Strait of Belle Isle, that I may luxuriate for a while in the vicinity of icebergs — those huge monsters of the deep which are at once our terror and delight. One can not go every where, however, in two months, so it was with a serene feeling of satisfaction that we saw the anchor tripped to the sailors' song, and jerked to the cat-head with the last word of the last line.

" Up with the jib !" cried the captain, with a certain gleeful ring in his tones. Then, turning to us, " Homeward bound, gentlemen ; our keel will soon be in Christian waters, and I shall be happy."

It was with a sad kind of feeling that we said our silent good-bye to the wondrous scenery that opened as we passed the mouth of Dartmouth River, for there is about such landscapes a grandeur all their own.

In the course of half an hour, for the wind was light, we rounded the ugly little boat that does duty as a light-ship, and in the course of the next hour had passed Douglastown, sending our farewell wishes ashore, and were making our way across Mal Bay.

" Rain, sure as you live," said Edwards, coming aft and pointing to a black mass of clouds in the southwest.

It was not a rain, but a pour. It seemed as though the bottom of the upper sea had suddenly dropped out, and let every thing through at once—a perfect wall of water was moving toward us. As the heavy drops fell in the smooth sea, they made a queer, dull, rushing sound, and in a few minutes every thing was drenched. Percè Rock and Bonaventura were only a couple of miles off, but they were entirely shut out from view.

That night, however, was a perfect marvel. The clouds had all disappeared with the setting sun, and the troops of stars came out one after another, until it seemed as though, even in infinite space, there was not room enough for all, and yet they continued to come out in innumerable hosts, making the heavens glitter with a million million points of light.

The wind was gentle, and just fanned us along, but at about eleven it freshened, and at one it rose to a gale. The top-hamper was all snugly stowed, but it became necessary to call all hands to reef the mainsail and take the bonnet off the jib.

We rushed by the Bay of Chaleur, and by daylight made Miscou. The wind grew stronger as the sun rose, and though we had planned to keep to the eastward of North Point, and sail through the pleasant waters of Northumberland Strait, stopping at Pictou for a day or two, we were driven so far out to sea that we were compelled to go back the same way we came, along the northern shore of Prince Edward's. We passed a large number of fishing schooners lying to under trysails, but managed to hold our course until we got under the lee.

It is not necessary to describe the home trip in detail. We sailed through the beautiful and quiet waters of the Gut of Canso, stopping at Port Mulgrave to get a huge package of letters, which were more cheering than can be imagined. Across Chedebucto Bay, and into the Little Gut of Canso next, where we anchored, as it was almost a dead calm. There we got ice, fish, and lobsters, and had made preparations to remain all night, when the water rippled to the eastward, foretelling a stiff breeze from that direction.

" I fear we are going to have a rough night," said the captain. " This wind comes up in an ugly sort of way, and my impression is we shall get a heavy blow before morning."

" Well, Cap, we can stand a blow as well as any one ; so get your anchor up and we'll be off."

" It won't be pleasant to run into an old-fashioned gale," he replied, " and it looks now as if we were going to have one."

I do not pretend to be weatherwise, but quite otherwise. I was anxious to get home, however, since we had started, and felt that if it were a three days' storm that was coming up, we could take the first end of it, and possibly get to Halifax before the gale had fairly got under way.

" No matter, Cap, let's get away and take our chances."

So off we went. When we were almost opposite Roaring Bull, the wind began to gather itself up for a hard rough-and-tumble blow. The breeze came in a hesitating sort of way, as though it were pushed along by an immense quantity behind, that had not yet shown itself or its power. The swell of the ocean began to break into white-caps, which after a while made one sheet of foam far as the eye could reach. I repented having given the order to get under way, and heartily wished myself safely at anchor again ; but regrets are always vain, and when one starts it is a bad sign to go back. A return was suggested, but it looked too much like a defeat, so I laughed at the croakings I heard, though I was as much afraid as any one, and promised in a boastful sort of way to take an early breakfast in Halifax the next morning.

At supper the yacht pitched so it was impossible to sit at table. Ah Boo braced himself as he poured the tea, and the gentlemen were compelled to hold their cups in their hands. Even then a sudden lurch would empty the cup completely, and tumble the victim of untoward circumstances on the nearest transom, or throw him against the partition of the state-room.

" Old Neptune is on his high horse to-night," said Bertric.

" Yes, we'll have all we want before morning," responded Ruloff.

" Humph, I've got more than I want now," said Stigand, as he dropped a cup of hot tea in his lap.

By ten o'clock it was as dark as pitch. It was cloudy and threatening rain, and the wind was blowing a perfect gale. It was fair though, coming in over the larboard quarter, so that we could rush along with start-sheets—and rush along we did. If ever a vessel felt herself in a hurry, the *Nettie* did that night. She brushed the water from her bows, and leaped like a thing of life from wave to wave.

> " There was music in her sail,
> As it swelled before the gale,
> And a dashing at her prow
> As it cleft the waves below ;
> And the good ship sped along,
> Scudding free."

" How fast, Cap ?"

" Well, a good twelve-knot."

" Good ; then my prediction will prove true, and I will eat my breakfast bacon in the Halifax Hotel at nine in the morning."

I got my wolf-robe, and had just made myself comfortable, when I heard—

" All hands on deck to reef the mainsail." You can easily see that it must be blowing hard, when with the wind on our quarter it became necessary to shorten sail ; but such was the case. Ten of us worked away

K 2

for as much as thirty minutes before the last reefing-point was tied, and then the yacht trotted along at a slashing pace, but with a much steadier gait.

We all went below and slept soundly until daybreak. At seven Edwards said to me—

" That's Chebucto Light, ten miles ahead of us."

" What do you mean ?". I replied. " If that is Chebucto Light, then we are not more than fifteen miles from Halifax."

" Just about fifteen," he replied, quietly. " Supper in Canso and breakfast in Halifax ; well, that will certainly do to put down in our log-book."

" Did you ever accomplish such a feat before, Edwards ?"

" No, and I don't want to again. I've been up all night, and the whole fore-deck has been one sheet of foam."

At nine o'clock we entered Halifax Harbor, and came to anchor. Just then the wind was blowing with such ferocity that it fairly lifted boards from a pile on a wharf near us, and flung them around in the most reckless manner. We had had enough of it, and were glad to get to a place of safety, for had we been out longer we should certainly have been blown to pieces. At noon it seemed as though all the furies were let loose at once. The city was filled with clouds of dust, and every once in a while we heard the crash of a shutter that had been broken off its hinges, and was being carried on a free expedition, while the slamming of doors was heard above the garrison band, and there were so many hats in the air that one could easily suppose it to be a gala occasion, on which every Englishman was making this demonstration in honor of his queen.

We remained in Halifax several days to have the yacht painted, and snugged up for the reception of friends at home. When we did start we were made thoroughly and unpleasantly acquainted with the traditional fogs, which love this shore so dearly that they seldom leave it. We had hardly left Sambro Light before we lost all view of the land. For two mortal days and nights we tumbled about in the ground-swell, without wind enough to keep us steady, and became so demoralized that we were nearly ready to sink into untimely graves for the sake of change. Once the fog lifted, and kindly permitted us to run for the night into Port Mouton, where we enjoyed a quiet anchorage, and a very unsuccessful search for any thing in the shape of bird or beast. At another time we ran close upon the rocks just off Shelburne Harbor, and escaped them only by putting the wheel hard down at the cry from the lookout—

" Breakers ahead !"

Shelburne Harbor, where we anchored that night, is one of the loveliest spots conceivable. The river is perhaps a mile wide, and very picturesque. For a summer residence it would be unequaled. The scenery is varied, in some places undulating and wooded, and in others rocky, abrupt, and rugged, with huge cliffs bending like giants over the sea, while the broad deep lies beyond in full view. I felt when I saw the hundreds of cords of drift-wood floating lazily down the waters of the Penobscot some years ago, what a pity it is that the poor people of New York live so far off.

They could have their winter's supply of wood for the asking. But, by some strange law, the people and the wood are so widely separated that they are of no use to each other. So I felt concerning the Nova Scotia real estate. There were head-lands, bluffs, huge rocks, not to be imitated by art. Woods, ocean, every thing in short to make property valuable, but nobody to buy, and nobody to enjoy it. These exquisite sites are so far removed from the people that they must needs be satisfied with the fever and ague of Staten Island. When we get the means of bodily transportation which corresponds with the transportation of messages by electricity, Nova Scotia will receive her just tribute of praise as one of the loveliest shores on the continent.

After leaving Shelburne, with its first-class light-house, perhaps the best on the coast, we ran for Sable Light, with Algar at the wheel. Every thing was moist and disagreeable. Our clothing felt as though it had been recently washed and imperfectly wrung out ; and we were ready for any thing in the way of a sensation. A light breeze gave us start-sheets, and the main-boom hung well outboard. All at once I heard a "By Jove" from Algar, as he put the helm up with all his might.

"What's the matter ?" I cried, jumping up and dropping the damp book I had been trying to read.

"Just look there," he answered, pointing to the port bow. "Breakers, as sure as you live."

I looked, and within twenty feet of the yacht was a huge black whale asleep. We passed so close to him that the end of the main-boom was over his back.

If we had run into him the public would have been

spared the infliction of reading this account, and a full dozen life-insurance policies would have suddenly come due.

Ruloff rushed on deck gun in hand, and let the fellow have a charge of No. 1 shot right in the hump. It did not probably hurt him seriously, but it evidently woke him up, for he slashed his flukes around in the most preposterous manner, making the white foam fly in the air like a snow-storm.

The next day we crossed the Bay of Fundy. We knew we must be in that locality, for in no other place do the waters make such a bobbery. The steady swell gave place to a most unpleasant chop sea, and the *Nettie* was so surprised at the new condition of affairs that she jumped about in a very disagreeably suggestive manner for twelve long hours, during which time we hardly knew whether to be sick or not, but maintained a dogged silence about our interior condition which left our meals uncared for and untouched.

The next day the sun came out—blessed sight!—and at noon we took our bearings. Edwards walked the deck to cogitate upon the various courses we had sailed, and the number of miles we had probably made, then descended to the cabin to put his prophetic finger on the spot on the chart where we actually were, or where we ought to be. This guess-work seemed a little marvelous to us landsmen, and we accepted his assertions with a large pinch of salt. John, however, had got his quadrant from his box, taken his observations, pulled his Bowditch from its hiding-place, and in half an hour, compasses in hand, pricked the exact point on the chart which at that moment the *Nettie* occupied.

"Where are we?" asked Edwards, who was willing to set his guess against all the nautical instruments in the world.

"Right there," answered John, pointing to a place twenty miles south-southeast from Manhegin.

"Right there, hey; well, let me see—I said we were there"—pointing to another place not seven miles by chart measurement from John's calculation.

The instinct of the true sailor is a very wonderful thing. It is a mystery to me how he can keep his reckoning so accurately. During the days and nights when we had been sailing in a fog, without a glimpse of land, Edwards had kept every tack in mind, the speed we had made, and the probable effect of the currents, and had guessed within seven miles of our exact position.

"We shall see land in an hour," he said, triumphantly, as he came up on deck. Not one of us believed a word of it. But before the hour was up the lookout cried from the maintop—

"Land ho!"

"Where away?"

"Two points off the starboard bow."

Then we could see in the dim distance a sort of haze on the horizon, which in fifteen minutes assumed the indistinct outlines of an island.

"What land is it?" I asked.

"Manhegin," replied Edwards.

And, sure enough, Manhegin it was.

All night we drifted toward Portland Lights, and in the morning passed Boone Island, headed for the Shoals. We had written from Gaspe that we would meet our friends at the Shoals on the fifteenth, Saturday; and by nine o'clock on the sixteenth, Sunday, we dropped anchor by the side of the *Idler* in front of the Appledore.

Three ladies are a serious matter on board a yacht; but three ladies and a small boy only five years of age, who is constantly leaning over the rail, or trying to climb the shrouds, and who requires at least four pairs of watchful eyes to see that he does not become food for the fishes, is certainly a very serious matter. I wonder more and more every year, however, that the ladies do not take possession of the fleet. It would be beneficial in every way. In the first place, it would make the cabin of the yacht more like home; and, in the second place, it would cultivate a love of healthful pleasure which is not hostile to the most delicate refinement. American women are notably wanting in physical culture. It is seldom we see robust and ruddy health in the other sex. The woman of American society knows more, is far more interesting, and is acknowledged to be handsomer—that is to my mind the most dignified word with which to express good looks—than her sisters in any part of the world, but it is rare to find one in perfect health. Sick-headaches and neuralgia, caused by over-cerebration, are among the most common complaints, and one hears of these troubles so frequently that he begins at last to feel that the diseases mentioned are among the original and normal elements of which the average woman is constituted.

The causes of this degeneration are visible to the most casual observation; too early entrance into society, overcrowding of the brain at school, a premature development of matrimonial ambitions, and no exercise at all.

If the wives of all yachtsmen would take possession of their husbands' craft, peaceably if possible, forcibly if necessary, and insist on sailing the main with their liege lords, a taste of out-door life might be diffused over the general public which would paint the pale cheeks of our girls with a ruddy richness which no rouge supplies, and create a public opinion in favor of health which would exorcise these ghosts and goblins of neuralgia and headache which haunt so many of our homes.

But I am too near the end of my voyage to begin to preach. I have kept out of the Sleepy Hollow of sermonizing so long that I will not yield to the instinct at this stage.

Nothing that need be mentioned happened on the home trip from the Shoals until the morning when we left that quaintest of all quaint places, Provincetown. We had landed there early in the afternoon, and had spent three or four hours in exploring the mysteries of its single street, in looking over the curiosities in its museum, in regarding the wonderful view to be had from the top of its only tower, and in recalling the various incidents connected with the landing of the Pilgrims on what Mrs. Hemans is pleased to call " a stern and rock-bound coast." Stern certainly it is, as we found to our sorrow the next day, but so far is it from being rock-bound that it is only defended by sand-bars, and a rock would be a natural curiosity.

Be it known that I had been especially careful to

select good weather for this trip, because I wanted the ladies to become acquainted with the sea in her most coy and joyous moods. I had in my mind's eye certain excursions to be developed in the future, which would seem very plausible to the feminine mind if their present voyage should present only smooth water and fanning breezes.

My heart sank within me, however, the next morning, when I found that the captain had weighed anchor, and that we were already beyond Race Point, and heading for the Highlands. The wind was blowing a stiff breeze, the Atlantic swell was rolling in, and once in a while curling up into white-caps, which made me fear that the only song to be sung that day would be " Home, sweet Home."

I began to remonstrate very vigorously with the captain for bringing us out in such weather, but he assured me that in a couple of hours at most we should be running along with a free wind, and that we should then feel very little motion. I rushed below, and persuaded my wife, who was just beginning to feel that peculiar dizziness which is premonitory of more vigorous and active symptoms, to hurry with her dressing at any cost, and get on deck at the earliest possible moment. Any delay would be fatal. She was in that suggestive condition when she seemed to think that it was hardly worth while to make any effort; but I pleaded and begged and besought, until the boots were buttoned and the hat was on. Then with uncertain gait she made her way on deck, where I had prepared, of wolf-skin and blankets, a cozy little nest out of the reach of the spray.

I mildly suggested breakfast in the most far off and remote way of which my vocabulary was capable, but the prompt and decided manner in which such a possibility as eating was received sealed my lips.

I did my best after that to get the other ladies on deck, but my efforts were vain. One lay still and silent, with closed eyes and a patient expression of suffering which indicated only too plainly that Father Neptune was putting on the thumbscrews. She was like those whom Donne describes so vividly, who,

> "Coffined in their cabins, lie equally
> Grieved that they are not dead."

The other, surprised and chagrined beyond expression at the possibility of sickness, with a determination which would supply a martyr with material to endure the blazing fagot, dressed in an intermittent sort of way, but in a way so very intermittent that she was not seen on deck until four o'clock in the afternoon.

Cape Cod is seldom an easy point to pass, but at this particular time the Old Atlantic seemed to be doing his best to make things uncomfortable. The wind blew furiously, and the sea had on a regular English Channel chop.

It made me a little indignant, however, that William, who had left his business to enjoy the home run with us, maintained such equanimity in the surge. It seemed no more than right that a landsman should be downright sick ; but, though once or twice his lips grew just a bit purple, he wheeled into line with the old sailors and laughed at the storm. To test him, I invited him below to lunch. For a single moment he hesitated, as though uncertain whether it were better to

> " Bear those ills we have
> Than fly to others that we know not of,"

and then descended to the depths, where he completely vindicated himself by eating a cold mutton-chop.

When we were in the trough of the sea, I, sitting in the cockpit, could not see the top of the Highlands, only a couple of miles to leeward. The water came on deck in such profuse quantities that every thing floated a part of the time, and the sailors were chiefly occupied in paddling after stray bits of property which were trying to get overboard.

I noticed several times that the water struck the lee boat—our best boat of course—with such force that she was lifted up a few inches, and then came down with a shock which bent the davits in a very disagreeable way. While the captain and I were standing together and talking of the prospects, he suddenly cried out—

" Just look there ! that lee boat is going !"

And, sure enough, her hour had come.

The forward line gave way, and she went down bows first. Why is it that every thing goes wrong end first in this life ? If that boat had dropped stern first we could have saved her. But she must needs go down bows first, in consequence of which, as we were going nine knots, she instantly filled with water, and then gave a wrench and twist to the other davit which made me feel for a moment that the whole rail would be torn off. We did our best to save her, but our efforts were as nothing in that heavy sea. At last I gave orders to cut her away, and the next minute she was floating astern. We had the gloomy satisfaction of knowing that every thing belonging to her—oars, thole-pins, backboard, sponges, etc.—were in her, and that whoever picked her up would get every thing that was needed for immediate use.

This little incident created quite a stir on board. My wife lost at once all signs of seasickness, and watched the proceedings with as steady a nerve as though she were standing on the land. The sufferers below heard the noise and the cries, and remarked that it made very little difference to them what was happening on deck; that they should neither be very much frightened nor yet very sorry if the *Nettie* herself should take it into her capricious head to go below. Then I knew that the matter was serious.

However, after a few hours of bad weather we ran into the Sound, and by four o'clock were snugly and safely anchored in the harbor of Edgarton, and this time in the pleasant company of the *Phantom*.

Nothing that need be mentioned happened after this, and we reached New York with very pleasant memories of the past.

The whole cruise to the St. Lawrence was one long delight, and I am looking forward to another trip, across Newfoundland—that unknown territory which has charms all its own.

Dear Reader, now that I have finished this very pleasant task, I feel that I have but poorly described the exquisite pleasure we all enjoyed as we passed through these varied experiences on sea and land. It only remains for me to hope that you will some day take the same trip; and may the summer sea have fair skies, and the hospitable people all along shore treat you with that unstinted kindness which, was meted out to us. I bid you all good-night, with the prayer that you may sing throughout the voyage of life the song of the poet—

> " How sweet to rove,
> With such a beaming sky above,
> O'er the dark sea, whose murmurs seem
> Like fairy music in a dream !
> No sound is heard to break the spell
> Except the water's gentle swell,
> Whilst midnight, like a mimic day,
> Shines on to guide our moonlit way."

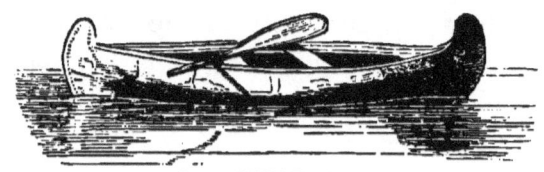

GEORGE ELIOT'S NOVELS.

LIBRARY EDITION.

ADAM BEDE. Illustrated. 12mo, Cloth, $1 50.

DANIEL DERONDA. 2 vols., 12mo, Cloth, $3 00. *(Vol. I. Ready.)*

FELIX HOLT, THE RADICAL. Illustrated. 12mo, Cloth, $1 50.

MIDDLEMARCH. 2 vols., 12mo, Cloth, $3 00.

ROMOLA. Illustrated. 12mo, Cloth, $1 50.

SCENES OF CLERICAL LIFE, and SILAS MAR-NER, The Weaver of Raveloe. Illustrated. 12mo, Cloth, $1 50.

THE MILL ON THE FLOSS. Illustrated. 12mo, Cloth, $1 50.

HARPER & BROTHERS *also publish Cheaper Editions* of GEORGE ELIOT'S NOVELS, as follows :

FELIX HOLT. 8vo, Paper, 75 cts.—*THE MILL ON THE FLOSS.* 8vo, Paper, 75 cents. — *MIDDLEMARCH.* 8vo, Paper, $1 50 ; Cloth, $2 00.—*ROMOLA.* 8vo, Paper, 75 cents.—*SCENES OF CLERICAL LIFE.* 8vo, Paper, 75 cents.—*SILAS MARNER.* 12mo, Cloth, 75 cents.

Few women—no living woman, indeed—have so much strength as "George Eliot," and, more than that, she never allows it to degenerate into coarseness. With all her so-called "masculine" vigor, she has a feminine tenderness, which is nowhere shown more plainly than in her descriptions of children. — *Boston Transcript.*

She looks out upon the world with the most entire enjoyment of all the good that there is in it to enjoy, and with an enlarged compassion for all the ill that there is in it to pity. But she never either whimpers over the sorrowful lot of man, or snarls and chuckles over his follies and littlenesses and impotence. — *Saturday Review,* London.

George "Eliot's" novels belong to the enduring literature of our country—durable not for the fashionableness of its pattern, but for the texture of its stuff. —*Examiner,* London.

PUBLISHED BY HARPER & BROTHERS, NEW YORK.

☞ *Either of the above books sent by mail, postage prepaid, to any part of the United States or Canada on receipt of the price.*

HARPER'S CATALOGUE.

Harper's Catalogue comprises a large proportion of the standard and most esteemed works in English and Classical Literature—COMPREHENDING OVER THREE THOUSAND VOLUMES—which are offered, in most instances, at less than one half the cost of similar productions in England.

To Librarians and others connected with Colleges, Schools, &c., who may not have access to a trustworthy guide in forming the true estimate of literary productions, it is believed this Catalogue, with its classified and analytical Index, will prove especially valuable for reference.

To prevent disappointment, it is suggested that, whenever books can not be obtained through a bookseller or local agent, applications with remittance should be addressed direct to Harper & Brothers, which will receive prompt attention.

Sent by mail on receipt of Ten Cents.

Address

HARPER & BROTHERS, FRANKLIN SQUARE, N. Y.